Desire's Anthem

A Rock 'N' Roll Romance

Samantha Egret

Desire's Anthem

www.chancespress.com
Chances Press, LLC
Las Vegas, NV

ISBN:0692345019

For R.C.

Overture

All she could hear was their heavy breathing. It was like time had stopped for the briefest of moments. Hannah Mercury opened her green eyes and gazed deeply into Connor's brown ones. He was stroking the bare skin of her breast methodically under her blouse, gently rubbing their already hard tips. It didn't matter that they were in his car. It didn't matter that right outside the windshield was a rusty old dumpster. It didn't matter that she was running late for her train, or that her husband and children were waiting at home for her to start the long weekend together. All that mattered was that he was next to her, at this moment, and that they had just shared their third intense kiss. She couldn't remember when she had felt so alive.

He paused. "Too much?"

She moaned, shaking her head. "Not enough—never enough." She felt her throat choke up, and leaned into his solid shoulder. The cotton of his shirt was surprisingly soft, and his cologne intoxicating. They sat there like that for a few minutes.

Finally, he drew in a deep breath. "It's getting late."

"I know."

"You can't miss the last train."

"Why not?" She rolled her head on his shoulder to look up at him. "I know, I know. You're right. But I don't want to go."

"We have to, Hannah. I can't drive you home again."

"I know." Tears formed in her eyes. She quickly wiped them away. "I'm sorry."

He started to drive out of the parking lot of the bar, and moved into traffic. Once they were underway, he placed his hand on hers. "Hannah, we can't go on like this any longer. You have to decide whether you want us to be friends or—something else. I'll do whatever you want me to do."

"I know, I know. You're right, I know." She sighed, pulling her blond hair behind her ears. "I want to be friends."

He glanced over at her. "Are you sure?"

She drew in her breath deeply. "Yes, I'm sure. It's what's right." She locked her fingers with his. They drove that way for the rest of the short ride to the train station. As he pulled into the loading zone, she felt an uncontrollable sense of dread.

He looked over at her. "Let me get the door for you, okay?" She nodded. He got out of the car and walked around to the passenger side.

Once he opened the car door, she got out and looked up at him. "We'll be better next week." She moved to grab her briefcase, but then stopped. She moved into his arms instead, and he lifted her into a tight embrace. She kissed his temple, and then he slowly eased her down. Connor reached into the car and pulled out her briefcase, then handed it to her. She slung the strap over her shoulder. "Okay—well—happy New Year."

"See you next year," he said, grabbing her hand one last time.

She forced back the tears that were formulating, and smiled up at him as he retained her hand. "We'll be better next year." Slowly, she walked away from him, and their hands touched until it was only their fingertips that barely brushed, and then nothing. Hannah could not push back the feeling that this was the last time she would ever see him like this. She looked back at Connor, waved, and then turned toward the train station.

*

The timing was off—it couldn't be helped. It didn't matter what he did, he just couldn't make it work. Danny Ayres rhythmically picked at the four strings under his fingers, in the hopes that it would somehow resolve this unfixable disaster of a tune, but everything he tried just seemed to accentuate how crappy it was. He threw off the headphones and kicked his guitar stand.

How could this be happening to him, the guy that had a new chord progression in his head every day since he could remember, even before he knew how to handle a guitar?

The first thought that came to his mind was what Gavin had said, about musicians writing all their best music in their twenties, and that everything after that was downhill. But Danny thought he'd dodged that bullet—he'd turned thirty-five last summer, and had been proud three years before to release an EP of songs under his Exquisite Corpse project. That had been a real accomplishment, to finally put together an album that reflected his vision as a musician. He and the guys had scrounged up enough money to record the songs, and when they were done with the mixing he'd known what they had was new and completely unexplored territory. They'd even sold a couple hundred copies within a few months on the internet. But then Curtis, the lead singer, had to go and get his girlfriend pregnant, dropping the band just days before they were scheduled to perform at the Roxy in front of a big exec Danny had convinced to stop by. They couldn't find a decent replacement in time. Not only was their show canned, but any chance at a recording deal, and Exquisite Corpse became a project that lived only in Danny's head.

Or at least he thought it still lived. But his recent slump in inspiration had him second-guessing. He stood up, rubbing his forehead. He just needed to focus, that was all. Focus.

The phone rang.

Shit. He really hoped it was not who he thought it was. But when he looked down at his phone, sure enough there was the drunken selfie they'd shot at the happy hour 6 months ago, which he'd allowed her to

place on his contacts. Oh, God. Another pain-ridden conversation with
Suzette was the last damn thing he needed right now. She'd gotten way
out of control, and his usual hints were not having any effect. He'd
ignored the last 5 calls, but he could tell that she just wouldn't leave him
alone until he said what he needed to say, straight up. He slid his finger
over the screen to answer. "Yeah?"

"Danny, why haven't you been picking up your phone? I've been
calling you all evening."

"Didn't feel like talkin'."

There was a dead silence on the other end. "You intentionally ignored me?"

"Pretty much."

More dead silence. "You know, Danny—I really don't appreciate
that."

He rolled his eyes. "If you stopped calling, I wouldn't have to ignore you."

Her voice rose to a high-pitched growl—the one that could always
be heard from the other side of the office. "I don't think you understand who you're dealing with."

"I know who I'm dealing with, but since I'm not on the clock right
now it doesn't matter. Please stop calling me."

More silence, with an undercurrent of labored breathing. "Danny, I
don't understand why you're treating me like this. I told you I loved
you."

"And I told you I wasn't into having a serious relationship. We
made a deal."

"But the last six months have been so intense. I thought you felt
what I felt." He could hear her sobbing on the other end. "You don't
know how vulnerable I am right now—what I'm capable of. All I need
to do is get a razor—"

"Jesus, Suzette—you need to be calling your shrink, not me."

Back to the growl. "Listen, asshole, I'm gonna make you wish you were never born, dick! Just wait for Monday morning. You will *never* work in the music industry again, never."

"Try threatening me, Suzette. Bottom line is that we're through." He hung up the phone. Time for damage control.

*

Now was the time to pull out all the stops. Danny's one advantage on Monday morning was that Suzette never came in before 10:00 a.m. He had two hours to convince Ned that he was what Unchained Records needed, not Suzette. The key was in the Androgynous Punk campaign—he and Suzette had been knocking it around for weeks, and he had been trying to convince her that the way to go was through more indie, non-corporate avenues. Suzette wanted to keep it 100% digital and web-based. But Danny knew that the wave of the future was incorporating the past. He had worked up a guerilla tagging campaign, canvased local coffee and tea bars and underground clubs in the major metropolitan areas, and gotten a real sense for how the target population discovered music—and it wasn't through digital music stores. Suzette had postponed the campaign twice now because of her dedication to tired ideas, and Danny had been thinking for weeks about going over her head. He knew Ned was getting impatient. It was now or never.

Running his fingers through his long, wavy, brown hair, Danny opened the door to Ned's office. His rugged good looks, his chiseled face with the perfectly maintained devil-may-care facial hair, wouldn't help in this—that's what he'd used to get ahead with powerful women like Suzette. He had alluring brown eyes, and when he set his thick eyebrows just so and smiled with his pouty lips, he could give a bedroom look that made any woman submit. But Ned was no woman, and

Danny had to use his quick wit and street smarts on this one, full blast. He cleared his throat.

Ned looked up from his computer, heavy rimmed glasses glaring off the screen, black hair and goatee perfectly manicured, as usual. "Danny—what've you got for me?"

"Ned, thanks for making time for me this morning."

"Just please tell me you have something for Androgynous Punk."

Danny drew in a deep breath and sat in a chair opposite. "The truth is, Ned—I've had something for Androgynous Punk for weeks. And I think it's really good. But Suzette has been—hesitant to move forward."

"I'm listening."

"Look, this band screams Indie Pop Punk—it's in the name, for Christ's sake! So we gotta push them through avenues that will hook them up with the young, hipster crowd: guerilla tagging, stripped-down flyers in the coffee bars, interest from the hottest DJs running the club circuits, vinyl records. It's gotta look indie, but have the power of Unchained's global reach. They gotta feel like they're not sourcing corporate, but then be able to Shazaam that shit right into their phones within minutes. That's what'll bring Androgynous Punk to where they need to be." He leaned back in his chair.

Ned considered what had just been said, crossing his arms. "What you are proposing is straight outta the '90s."

"Ummm, yes and no. You see, we utilize outreach methods reflective of that time, because the target audience idealizes that as nostalgia—" he saw Ned raise an eyebrow, "—inconceivable to us as that may be. But we keep this band at the top of every Google search with a full-on blast to the top websites and Indie rock blogs. I'm talkin' TMZ and Mofo on Music. I'm talkin' Facebook and Twitter. We take it to the streets, but we re-route those streets while we're doin' it. We make every local hipster community think that this band is one of theirs. That's the only way to make Androgynous Punk totally legit in their eyes." Danny leaned back again, glad that he'd been drilling these same points to Suzette for weeks.

Ned nodded his head. "Play their game, but change the rules. Yes—I like it. How ready is this to go?"

"We can have it on the streets in a week, but give me two and I'll have the web buzz going, too. I've been ready to pull the trigger on this thing, I just need you to say go."

"Ned!" Suzette's voice made them both jump slightly in their seats. She stormed into Ned's office, dressed in the red suit she always wore on a firing day.

"Suzette, glad you're here early—Danny was just telling me about this raw new campaign for Androgynous Punk."

"Oh God, Ned, that's why I'm here early. We need to talk—alone." She hadn't even looked Danny's way.

Ned raised his eyebrows. "Great. Danny, in the meantime—yes. I want you to get a move on making this thing real. I'm saying go."

Danny stood up. "Thanks, Ned. I'll make it happen." He reached over and shook Ned's hand.

Ned grabbed his hand and slapped his shoulder. "I know you will. That's why I'm putting you directly in charge of the Androgynous Punk campaign."

Suzette leaned into Ned's desk. "Ned, I don't think we should move on this until I have a chance to talk to you."

Ned gave a terse glance to her. "Suzette, this is happening. Danny's taking over this campaign, and every other indie-type act that we have, for that matter. I've been nervous about the delays on this thing. I think you're just too far stretched. From here on in, Danny will report directly to me."

Suzette's voice rose again to its highest pitch. "Ned, I think we should talk first…"

"And I'm saying it's done. I have a new dream team. You ready to play ball, Suzette?"

Suzette set her shoulders, clearly livid and directing her speech at Ned. "We need to talk."

Danny cleared his throat. "Ned, thanks for your confidence in me—you won't be sorry." He turned to leave.

"Great, Danny—we'll talk later."

Danny cleared the room and didn't stop until he was in his own workspace. He let out a relieved sigh as he sat in his own chair, even as he could hear Suzette screeching across the office.

Track 1

Androgynous Punk had taken off in a big way. Not only did the hipster crowd welcome them with wide open arms; the radio stations had glommed onto them, too. In fact, the past year had taken them from indie to mainstream so quickly, that they were starting to lose a little bit of legitimacy with their fan base. A lot of the buzz on Twitter was that they had sold out. Danny knew it was time for another campaign. He pondered ideas while he looked out the window of what used to be Suzette's office.

Danny's sex life had taken off in a big way, too. Although he made a point to avoid hooking up with anyone from work (Suzette had taught him the folly of that enterprise), he still managed to meet plenty of hot women of all ages that were into exactly what he was: right now. Danny thought about the one last night: Brianne. Man, did she make him crazy. They'd met the week before at the gym—Danny had been working on tamping down his steadily growing beer belly (thirty-six sucked where physical fitness was concerned). At first she seemed a little standoffish. But when they started talking and she found out he worked full-time in the music industry and played in a band after-hours, things clicked right away. They always did—chicks liked the glamour of the whole industry concept. She'd been a cheap date, too. Just beer and a burger at Stout, and she was ready to go. They ended up at her place, and he ate her out while she sucked him 'til he popped. Didn't even have to bother with a condom. What she'd lacked in skill she'd more than made up for in resolve—and appetite. Oh, well—what more did he want from a twenty-five-year-old?

Truth was, the whole one-night stand thing was beginning to feel pretty empty. Even Gavin had met his special "one", Lydia. Danny was on board to be the best man in a few months. And he had to admit, despite himself and the concern that Gavin's wedding plans would ruin the progress of their new musical enterprise, Lydia was a real sweetheart. It must be nice to have someone to go out with, and know that you didn't have to be "on" the whole time. Hell, it must be nice to have someone to come home to.

His thoughts were interrupted by a brisk knock. Ned opened his office door. "Hey, Danny, someone I want you to meet." He waved someone in.

It was like he woke up at that moment. Her long, black hair shined from the lights of the office, and her perfectly oval face was set off by large, almond-shaped eyes. A tiny bow mouth was accentuated by bright lipstick. She was the most beautiful woman he'd ever seen up close.

"Danny, I want you to meet Akie Yamamoto, our newest marketing specialist. She's joining us from Unchained's Tokyo office. She'll be handling all the international campaigns." A slight frown played on Danny's face, but he was able to cover it almost as soon as he felt it. Suzette's replacement. He didn't think they were going to replace her this late in the game. Despite the success of Danny's indie acts, Unchained was still operating at a loss this year. He'd figured they'd continue to have him handle all the international accounts, as he had done since Suzette's departure. He wasn't sure why they were making a push to bring someone new on, international marketing chops or not.

Pushing these thoughts to the back of his head, Danny got up and held his hand out to Akie. As he approached her, he was taken by her stately presence—probably about 5'7". "Hope you like it here, Akie."

She took his hand and smiled. "Thank you, Danny. I'm glad to be here." He was surprised that she had no accent.

"How long have you been back in the States?"

"This is my first week back. I was in Tokyo for 5 years, but I actually grew up off Sawtelle," answered Akie, referencing the Japanese neighborhood in West Los Angeles. She looked like she had to explain that a lot to white dudes she met.

He tried to give her a look that showed he got it. "I live over there myself, actually right off of Selby."

"Oh," she said, nodding and obviously trying to look like that mattered. He had to admit to himself, it was sorta lame to bring that up—like that made them best buddies now. But while he was conflicted at the idea of possible competition from Akie, he was also sure that he wanted to get to know her better. His rule about dating a co-worker might need to be broken for this one.

*

Hannah looked down at her notes. She should have known the Council Member from District 12 would want to know why the new fire station was being put in the neighboring district and not his. She had put so much information together on the selected site that she had failed to organize her file of the sites that were rejected. Her Division Manager looked over at her expectantly as she nervously shuffled the papers.

"We, uh, did a cost comparison of multiple sites in the neighborhood, which as you know borders the two Council Districts. In the end, though, we decided that the selected site was the most advantageous as to cost and traffic flow."

The Council Member still didn't look satisfied. "And how much more expensive were acquisition costs expected to be in my district?"

She heard Connor's voice from the other side of the row of seats their staff occupied. "Sir, as you know, property costs increase dramatically north of Roscoe Boulevard. Properties in your Council District that were available and appropriate for a project of this scope were double of those in 3. So it really was a matter of going with the site that would allow us to put a higher budget towards construction."

"I see," said the Council Member, nodding his head. Hannah leaned over to give Connor a grateful look, but he didn't allow her to catch his eye. He just looked straight ahead.

Such had been the case for almost a year now. He seldom acknowledged her outside of the office, and even when in the office only communicated via e-mail or phone. If she happened to see him approaching while in the main walkway, he'd abruptly turn toward another aisle of cubicles. It was as if they had never shared those two precious months—actually, it was worse. At least he was amiable when he barely knew her. Now that he had known more of her, it seemed it was everything he could do not to turn away in utter and complete disgust. Her heart broke anew every day.

Things at home hadn't been much better. That night she'd come home from her last outing with Connor had also been the night she'd confided everything to her husband. He was sympathetic at first, hurt—shell-shocked. He'd tried to understand why what happened did, and obviously with the children in the next room couldn't lose it too much. But as the weeks progressed, and what had happened had sunk in, he became more distant, melancholy, and defeatist. He expressed that he just didn't trust her anymore, and couldn't feel like they were true partners, though they still shared the same bed and went through the same life routines that they had before. He had moved into the extra bedroom, and they were progressing through life as a family for their children, though as a couple it looked like they were probably through.

When Hannah had told Connor about confiding in her husband, he'd shut down completely. He expressed that he wasn't sure why he was spending time with her at all, since he already had a girlfriend and didn't need any more friends. That last part probably hurt the most, when she'd been so convinced they could emerge from this whole

experience with their friendship still intact. Afterwards, he had apologized, but the damage was already done. They had tried to coordinate a
few group outings with other co-workers, but it always felt awkward and
unnatural, trying to act like casual acquaintances when they had been so
much more. After those attempts, he'd stopped joining the groups; and
she had begun to feel timid to even approach him. He, to whom she'd
confessed some of her deepest emotions. It wasn't long before she
started to resent seeing him spending time with other female coworkers,
and an uncontrollable sense of betrayal permeated every interaction, to
the point where even speaking niceties had become impossible without
an undercurrent of tension. He had started avoiding her altogether.
Even today, when a group of five staff had been scheduled to attend the
Council Meeting at City Hall, Connor had opted to go separately, ahead
of the group.

Hannah returned to her office and her workspace, mentally exhausted from the morning.

"How'd it go?" asked Tammy, her best work friend, who had a habit
of calling questions out over the cubicle partitions.

Hannah dropped her purse onto her desk, then walked over to the
adjoining cubicle. Tammy was painting her nails, curly brown hair piled
high on her head, and a stack of files in her inbox happily ignored.
Hannah smiled, shaking her head slightly. "Tammy, you crack me up."
Tammy winked, her brown eyes sparkling from her jovial face, then re-
focused on her task. Hannah continued. "They approved the site and
gave us authority to draw up the plans and specs. No thanks to me, by
the way."

Tammy looked up from her nails. "Oh, no—what happened?"

"I got all tongue-tied when CD12 asked about the site selection process. Luckily, Connor had it together about the overall cost and saved
the day."

Tammy rolled her eyes. "Whatever. That's his job, to know financ-
es and stuff." Tammy refused to hear anything good about Connor
these days, being well-versed in what went down with Hannah. "So,
what's next?"

"Well, I gotta work with the Project Engineer and Architectural.
Council wants us to come back with the finished drawings and a full
estimate before approving the project for bid."

"That's unusual," said Tammy, finishing her nails. She lifted a robust arm and started to blow on her fingertips. "So what's for lunch?"

*

Danny tried to hide his frustration, for Ned's sake. "Look, we still
gotta legitimize this band with their base. It's damage control time."

Akie shook her head. "Sorry, how is being on the brink of international success damage? They've hit the mainstream in a big way. If the
hipster crowd can't deal with it, I say too bad and good riddance.
Unchained doesn't have time to waste on such a small percentage of the
population, and we don't have to justify ourselves to anyone. Neither
does Androgynous Punk." She turned to Ned. "I say we focus all we've
got on the international tour. These guys are going to hit it big in
Tokyo. They already have the look and the sound. Fuck Silverlake. We
can have these guys known as far as Iwami Ginzan." She looked at
Danny. "That's a silver mine in Japan."

"Yeah, I know what that is," (he didn't), "But I'm telling you, we
have to keep these guys on the pulse of their American crowd, too.
They gotta have something to come home to." He looked over at Ned.

Ned shook his head. "Sorry, Danny. I agree with Akie. We don't
have time to apologize for these guys. I'm moving the Androgynous
Punk campaign to Akie, effective immediately. Why go hipster when we
can go Harajuku?" He gave the look that indicated they were done, and

Danny and Akie filed out. He tried to cut over to his office without small talk—he was too pissed at losing Androgynous Punk, the band he'd help bring up in the first place. But Akie followed him.

"Look, it wasn't my intention to take on Androgynous Punk."

Danny kept walking. "Really? Coulda fooled me."

"Danny, I'm not trying to undermine you. I really just think that we need to keep Unchained going strong in the biggest markets. You've seen the financial reports just like I have, and at this point we all have to be in the same camp. We have to make this thing stay alive. Come on." Danny stopped and turned to her. She was smiling at him, long hair draping over her breast and accentuating the small amount of cleavage her blouse showed. "Can we collaborate on it? Transition them over so we both win?"

Danny sighed. "Look, I got too much on my plate right now. If Ned says AP is yours, they're yours. I don't got time to hold your hand through it."

"Can we at least talk about it over drinks? I know that what you initially did with their campaign hit in a big way. It would be nice to not have to start from scratch."

Danny looked at her again. She smiled at him with those perfect lips, and he knew he couldn't say no. "All right—where do you wanna go?"

*

They planned to leave directly from the office. Akie was being very agreeable—Danny guessed because she wanted him to stop feeling threatened by her. They agreed they'd head out together, and then Danny would take her back to her car after.

Akie settled into the passenger seat of his SUV. "So, where should we go? My knowledge of Hollywood night spots is over 5 years old."

"There's a good place off Sunset. They have a decent happy hour, and we can sit out on the patio and talk shop until you feel ready to run with it."

"Sounds good to me"

They headed over to the place and found a comfortable spot to talk. At first, their conversation was strictly around the campaign. But it wasn't long before the drinks set in, and they were talking about everything else.

"So, Danny—I've heard a lot about you. I wonder if all the rumors are true." Akie leaned over, smiling enticingly at him.

"What rumors do you hear?"

"That you're a male slut. That you fucked around with that Suzette chick, and that's why she left the company." She was smiling the whole time she said it.

Danny laughed. "I don't know about being a male slut. I mean, I like women. But, yeah—I had a thing with Suzette. But she left because she couldn't deal, not because of me."

"Isn't that just a different way of saying the exact same thing?"

"Look, I told her what the deal was at the time. I didn't want to be tied down. But she couldn't be okay with that, and so when I broke things off she threatened to fire me. I had to act fast to make sure Ned saw me as more than just Suzette's flunky. And it's a good thing I did, otherwise Androgynous Punk would still be playing in bar patios in Echo Park." He finished off his bourbon.

"Sounds like quite the power play." Akie was leaning over the table now, and he noticed that the top button of her blouse had come undone. Her black bra peeked out, and her cheeks were flushed bright red.

"I did what I had to do." He could feel himself focusing less and less on the memories of Suzette, and more on that unbuttoned blouse and what lay beneath. "You want another drink?"

Akie looked down at the unfinished Moscow Mule. "No, I should probably head back now. We still have work tomorrow."

"All right." He got up out of his seat, and Akie stood on the other side. He could tell she was a little shaky. He went over and offered his arm.

"Thanks. I guess it's been awhile since I drank this much." She took his arm, and they walked out of the patio and toward where his car was parked. As he opened the door to the passenger side, he noticed another button starting to come undone. His hand flew up to save it, but then he let his fingers fall in the crevice between her breasts, which were soft and deeply curved. Still flushed, she looked up at him, and then plopped into the seat, out of his reach. Right. Probably not a good idea.

Once Danny was settled into the driver's side, he reached to start the car, but then felt Akie grab his neck and pull him toward her. They were kissing drunkenly and passionately, and before he knew it both were grabbing at body parts. He plunged his tongue into her perfect mouth, and although they were out of sync, she still tasted amazing. His mouth left her lips and moved down her neck, and in between those two amazing tits. His tongue reached in, and he heard her moan. He grabbed underneath her, and started to pull up at her tight work skirt, until he could feel her soft skin underneath. With one move, he pushed her panties out of the way and started to knead at her luscious ass.

"Oh, Danny," she moaned.

He took that as a cue, and moved his hand around to the other side, cupping her crotch and plunging his middle finger into her tight little cunt. Wow, she was tight and dry—he imagined that it must feel amazing to have more than a finger plunged into that soft little heaven. As he imagined, he wiggled his finger around frantically, trying to find the spot that would make her scream, get her wet.

"Danny," she whispered.

"Jesus, you feel good." He moved his mouth back to hers, digging into the depths of her mouth with his tongue while his finger continued to explore her tighter end.

She moved her head back from his. "Danny…"

"I'm gonna make you scream…"

"Danny," Akie said, pushing his hand away from between her legs. "I think we should stop." She gently pushed him away from her and straightened her skirt. "I don't think drunk and in a parking lot is the way I want it to be."

He settled back into his seat and adjusted himself. "Right. Sorry." He looked over at her. "You just seemed so hot and ready."

She moved her hand through her hair and buttoned her blouse. "I really want to, Danny, but I think we should wait. After all, we haven't even had a real date yet."

He smiled at her. "I'm addictive, huh?"

Akie laughed. "Well, dinner would be nice."

"When?" Danny smiled over at her, tracing his finger around her lips and stroking her silky hair. "Give me a time and a day and I'll take you on the most amazing date ever."

*

There was no getting around it. He had fallen hard.

After that first hot and heavy night, Danny had taken Akie for a romantic dinner and then to the Magic Castle, an invite-only hotspot in Hollywood for enjoying magic (compliments of Gavin, who knew a guy). They'd gotten pretty worked up after, but she only let him get as far as he had before, and then bid him good night at the door to her complex. Danny suffered an uncomfortable ride back to his place, then choked one off as soon as he'd gotten through the door.

Every date after that for the next three months had been pretty much the same deal, although last time she had dug her fingers into his pants and given him a mini-hand job. She wasn't very good at it and she'd stopped before he could come, but he didn't really care. What she lacked in expertise was trumped by how much he wanted her, and the force with which he came later, once he took care of business alone by himself, was a testament to that.

And now she had agreed to travel up to Napa with him this weekend, as his date for Gavin and Lydia's wedding. He got hard just thinking about all the kinky things he would do to her once they were in the suite of that little remote bed and breakfast. He hoped the walls to the place were thick, or they were bound to disturb the other guests.

Friday afternoon before the Saturday wedding, Danny knocked on Akie's office door. She didn't answer, so he gently opened the door. She sat at her desk, typing away furiously. "Ready to go?"

Akie looked up from her typing, as if she'd just noticed him there. "Oh, Danny—you're going to kill me."

"What's going on?"

"There is a big clusterfuck-in-progress with the AP tour promotion. I have to make some serious phone calls to make sure things are on the right path before I can leave…"

"I don't like the sound of this."

Akie looked at him apologetically. "I have to figure this out, Danny. I can't leave with you tonight."

"We can leave in a few hours, and I should still be able to make it for the rehearsal dinner." He looked at her hopefully.

"No, Danny—you're the best man. You have to be there for the actual rehearsal." Danny groaned. "I promise—I *promise* I will drive up tomorrow morning."

"The ceremony starts at 1:00."

"I will be there, Danny." She got up from her desk and pressed her body against his. "And I will make it worth the wait."

*

It was probably for the better that Akie couldn't make the rehearsal. Danny hadn't even realized how much had to happen for a wedding to go off, and most of the evening was focused on making sure the ceremony was falling into place. Once they'd had the rehearsal dinner and Danny had done his part to entertain Gavin's family and their mutual friends, he was exhausted. He fell into bed, knowing that he wanted to be well-rested for the ceremony—and for after.

The next morning was busy with helping Gavin wake up on time, get ready on time, and stay calm enough to go through with the whole thing. Danny didn't even notice Akie's absence until he looked down at his watch and realized that it was time to head outside to the vineyard. The ceremony was starting in a half hour. He quickly texted Akie to see if she was near, but he knew that spotty coverage and her simple need to focus on the road would prevent a response. He headed to the altar, hoping he'd see her in the crowd.

It was the moment that he was passing the ring to Gavin that he saw her sneaking into the back row. She looked amazing in a yellow sundress, and the backlight of the sun showed off her figure under its thin material.

He almost dropped the ring.

The rest of the ceremony went off without a hitch, though, and once the bride and groom had been pronounced man and wife, everyone was able to mill about as they pleased. He headed straight to Akie. "You look amazing."

"Thanks, Danny—I hope I didn't disturb the ceremony too much."

"Naw, you just had me so hypnotized I almost forgot to hold on to the ring."

Akie laughed. "Well, I'm glad it all turned out okay in the end. This is a beautiful place for them to start their life together."

"Come on, I want you to meet them." Danny pulled Akie toward the newly-hitched bride and groom. "Gav, Lydia—someone I want you to meet."

Gavin slapped Danny on the shoulder. "I figured this was the one you haven't stopped talking about, at about the same time you almost dropped Lydia's ring at the sight of her."

Lydia laughed. "Geez, Danny—you had one thing to do, one thing!" Everyone burst into laughter. She held her hand out to Akie. "We are so happy to finally meet you—Danny really has nothing but glowing compliments for you."

Akie smiled. "Thank you both so much for letting me join you." She directed her next comment to Lydia. "You look beautiful."

"Six months on Weight Watchers later, but Gav assures me he likes 'em meatier."

Gavin reached over and grabbed his new bride. "The more Mrs. to love the better!"

They all laughed as the two newlyweds basked in each other's company. Lydia turned away for a second. "Danny, we're going to take some photos of the wedding party before the reception begins."

"Gotcha. Akie, will you keep me company?" He held out his hand again.

Akie took it. "I have absolutely nowhere else to be."

The rest of the afternoon was a blast. They drank and danced, and Danny and Gavin even unveiled their yet-to-be named band to the guests. Gavin serenaded Lydia while Danny strummed an acoustic guitar. Danny couldn't have hoped for a better way to sendoff his buddy into the unchartered territory of married life.

Finally, the party was over. But Danny knew that for him, the party was just beginning. He led Akie to his suite on the grounds. "I think you'll be pleased with the accommodations," he said as he pulled her through the door. The fireplace was already blazing, thanks to the tip he had given the housekeeper earlier. March evenings were still cold in Napa, despite the sunny days. The hot-tub was filled with sudsy water, and candles surrounded it. A bottle of wine waited for them to pop it open.

"Wow, this place is amazing!" Akie looked over at him. "You really pulled out all the stops, didn't you?"

Danny didn't answer—he just pulled her into his arms, his tongue pulling her mouth apart. She let out a small moan. He bit at her lip, and then moved his tongue over to her ear. "I've been wanting to tear that flimsy little dress off you all day," he whispered. "I could see your nipples through the fabric when the light was right."

"Oh, no, Danny—if you could see, that means everyone else could, too!"

"They'd have to be looking really close, and I wouldn't let anyone else get that close to you." He moved his lips down her neck, along her collarbone, and pulled the straps down as he tugged hard at the scooped neck. Two perfectly large, round breasts popped out. "Yes!" he said, filling each hand with one. He squeezed, pulling his fingers over those nipples that had been torturing him all day, squeezing each one 'til they were raw.

Akie took a sharp intake of breath. "Don't you think we should enjoy that hot-tub first?"

Danny nodded, then kneeled down in front of her. He gave a tug to the bottom of her dress, and it fell in a heap around her strappy sandals. He kissed her ankles, then worked his way up the inner part of her leg, up her thighs, until finally his lips rested outside of her silky panties. He pulled them down impatiently, pressing his lips against her neatly manicured pussy. Moving his fingers up to pull open the lips, he thrust his tongue towards her clit. He flicked his tongue for a few moments before he looked up and said, "Don't you think I can get you wet without the bath?"

Akie gave a shaky laugh. "I think I want to enjoy everything that the accommodations have to offer." She stepped out of the pile of clothing at her feet, reached down to pull off her sandals, and then pulled him into the bathroom. She stepped over the edge, and then lowered herself into the tub.

She watched as Danny unbuttoned his shirt, threw it to the floor, and then fumbled hastily with his pants. His sizable and erect penis burst out, and he pushed his pants down to the floor, along with his briefs. "Will you suck it?"

Akie gave a little smile, then placed her hands around his cock, pulling him toward her. She kissed the tip seductively, but then stopped short of any real blow job action and leaned back in the hot-tub. "Danny, I want you in the hot tub with me."

Danny shrugged to himself. Maybe blow jobs weren't her thing. Anyway, he wasn't going to let that stop him from having his way with this wet goddess that lounged in front of him, breasts bobbing in the water. He stepped into the tub, mounting himself over her as his head reached her mouth for another kiss. "I wanna take you right now." He reached down to guide his tool into that tight little cunt, thrusting his way in. She drew in her breath again. "Feels good, doesn't it?"

She held tight to him. "Um-hmm." Her eyes were closed, her lips pressed tight. He knew they'd make heat together. He thrust harder, pulled out, then thrust again. With each thrust she gave a short little moan.

"You feel so fucking good," he growled. He thrust again, and the water started sloshing around them.

"Maybe we should move to the fireplace?" she asked.

"Yeah," he agreed, pulling himself out and stepping out of the bath. He grabbed her hand and helped her out.

She reached for a towel. "We can put it underneath us." She stepped into the bedroom and placed the towel in front of the fireplace. He followed behind, and once the towel was down he grabbed her and flipped her facing upwards. Falling over her, he pried her legs apart and then thrust himself back into her. Another of her little moans.

"I'm glad we're outta the bath, 'cause now I have a lot better leverage." He smiled at her and pushed her legs up over her shoulders. "You are like a wet dream come to life." He pulled away and then thrust back in. He made sure his knees were positioned right, then pounded back into her repeatedly. Faster and faster he pounded, and he could feel her taut little cunt pulling at his cock. She was breathing shallowly. He rode like he hadn't ridden before, and pretty soon he felt what he'd been waiting to feel for months. "I'm gonna—" and then he burst into her.

"But, Danny," she said breathlessly, "We didn't use a condom."

He shuddered over her, only half-hearing the sense of urgency in her voice. "That's all right, you're on the pill, right?" He fell onto her, and she moaned a little. He could feel her lips kiss his cheek as he fell asleep on her.

The next thing he realized, he was waking up on the floor, and the sun was peeking through the thick drapes of the suite. He blinked, then saw Akie shrugging on a sweater. "You going somewhere?"

Akie looked over at him and smiled. "I have to get back to L.A. Too much to do to take another day off."

He lifted himself onto his elbows, into a sitting position. "You sure you don't wanna stick around, do a wine tasting or something?"

"No, I had plenty of wine yesterday." She reached for her purse. "But I'll see you on Monday?"

Danny got up and gathered her into his arms. Her body against his made him start to go hard again. "Suit yourself, but if you stay I have plenty of non-alcoholic treats for you."

She let out a little laugh. "Tempting, but I think the AP promotion is on the right track, and in Japan it's already Monday. The drive home will give me just enough time before my Tokyo team gets to the office." She gave him a quick kiss on the lips. "It was fun."

Danny smiled. "Alright—see you on Monday."

*

Danny couldn't stop thinking about what an amazing time he'd had with Akie. And it wasn't just the sex. They'd laughed together, enjoyed the company of his friends. They'd done all the things that couples do, and he hadn't been bored once. Danny never thought of himself as the settling type—but then again a life with Akie hardly felt like settling.

As he drove back to L.A., Danny also thought about how hard she'd been working on the Androgynous Punk promotion in Tokyo. It was like she was worried for her job.

And why shouldn't she be? Rumors had been flying for months now that Unchained couldn't sustain much longer without deep cuts to personnel. He knew that, even though Akie had been with the Tokyo office for five years before joining the L.A. team, she was also the newest of the higher-paid employees. If anybody was going to end up with a pink slip come Friday, it was her. Danny didn't know what that would mean for their relationship—and even though he'd known her only three months, he knew he didn't want her to be out of his life.

An idea began formulating in his head, and the more he thought about it the more he realized what a perfect solution it was. He pushed the gas a little harder, eager to get home.

*

Everything was perfect. Danny had invited Akie to his place before dinner Monday night. He'd made reservations at the trendiest new place on the Westside, but he wanted to make sure that the dinner would be a celebratory one. He had the champagne ready, but hadn't had enough time to bother with a ring. It didn't matter. He figured she was probably the kinda woman that would want to pick her own. And he would gladly buy her whatever kind of ring she wanted. At 7:00 p.m. exactly she knocked on his door.

When he opened the door she smiled at him, beautiful in the black pants and tailored shirt she'd worn to work that day. "Sorry I didn't have time to change before coming. I had a few left over issues to deal with."

"No worries—you look great no matter what you wear."

She stepped in to his living room. "You know, maybe we can just keep it casual tonight."

Danny shook his head. "You look fine—I'm sure you'll knock the socks off of everyone there. Getting reservations for this place last-minute was no easy task."

"Then cancelling them shouldn't be an issue." He looked at her questioningly. "I'm sorry, Danny—I just don't have the energy for a full-course meal tonight. Maybe we can do something really easy, like ramen on Sawtelle, or Hurry Curry."

Danny shrugged. "It's up to you. I just wanna be with you."

Akie smiled. "That's so sweet of you."

"Look, we can go beer budget for dinner, but you have to let me pour you some champagne before we head out. After all, we didn't get to do that wine tasting in Napa."

She laughed. "Champagne would be wonderful. I could use something to take the edge off of today."

"Great," said Danny, grabbing her hand. "Just come and sit over here on the couch, and I'll be back in a sec." He quickly popped the champagne and poured a few glasses, then walked into the living room and sat next to her on the couch. He lifted his glass. "To us."

She clinked his glass. "To us keeping our jobs, right?"

He swigged back some of the champagne. "You know, Akie, I've been thinking a lot about that. And I think we're better facing these possible layoffs as a team." He put his glass down on the coffee table and moved to kneel down on the floor in front of her. Her mouth popped open. "Akie, will you marry me?"

She put her hand to her heart. "Oh, Danny—I don't know what to say..."

"Yes is a good start." He smiled at her.

Akie shook her head. "Danny—I like you a lot. We had—a lot of fun over the past few months. But I'm in no place where I want to marry anybody. We hardly know each other."

"What more is there to know?" Danny was still on his knees.

"So much more, Danny. Like family and life goals and all sorts of things. You have no idea whether you even want the same things as I do!"

"I want you."

"Danny, I'm sorry if anything I said or did made you think that I was looking for any sort of long-term commitment from you. But there is no way my answer can be anything but no." She put her champagne glass down and sat back in the couch awkwardly. Danny got up off his knees and stood up. How could he have read this so wrong? "It's probably not a good idea for us to go on with that dinner. I'll go." She got up, grabbing her purse and heading toward the door, but turned when she got there. "I hope this doesn't mean we can't be friends."

Danny looked over at her, but couldn't meet her eyes. "Sure, yeah."

She smiled. "I'm glad. You're a fun guy, Danny." She looked down and then turned to open the door and leave.

Danny didn't stop feeling numb all week. He went through meetings like he was sleepwalking. He had conversations that he couldn't remember. The only thing he could think of was where he went wrong, and why he had allowed himself to come on so strong and fall so painfully hard. When Ned called him into his office Friday afternoon, he was still going through all the ways that he could've done things better. And he barely heard anything until the words "Sorry, but we're going to have to let you go," found their way to his ears.

He looked up out of his haze. "I'm being cut?"

"Sorry, Danny. You do good work, really you do. I've never met anyone else that can make people of all kinds just talk to them unedited. But your strength is in smaller pushes, and right now Unchained needs to focus on big. We don't have the money to spend on small. I'm sorry, my friend."

First Akie and now his job. How could a week that started out in heaven end up in hell?

Track 2

"Have you seen the new PR Specialist?" Tammy gulped her coffee. "What a hottie. He looks just like Jon Snow."

Hannah almost spat out her oatmeal with laughter. She quickly swallowed. "No comment—and no. But, honestly, I don't really care if he's hot or not. I just need him to build public approval for the new fire station."

Tammy shook her head. "All work and no play..."

"...makes me not have another Connor on my hands." She took a sip of her tea. They'd been able to expedite the drawing up and cataloging of the plans, and the preparation of the specs. But when they'd gone back to Council, a group of 40 residents had protested the new site, claiming that the noise was going to disrupt an otherwise perfectly quiet neighborhood, and that the neighborhood council had never been contacted regarding the project. Council suspended moving forward, until further assessment could be conducted. Management had quickly schemed that the best way to resolve the problem was not by changing the project, but by hiring someone to make the neighborhood think they'd had a chance to provide input. They'd filled that PR job quicker than she'd ever seen them fill a position—and, as seemed to be an alarming new trend for the City, had hired someone from the private sector, a marketing hotshot from the music industry. Eduardo said it would be easier to get approval for an exempt position that was deemed temporary—but Hannah guessed that someone not familiar with public policy would probably be more moldable—less likely to default to advocating for the people, more likely to fall in line with the needs of the project. And from what she'd heard, this guy was supposed to be a genius at getting buy-in from less cooperative populations. She hoped that all the rumors were true—otherwise, they'd lose funding on the fire station and have to start from scratch. "I guess I'll get a chance to meet him tomorrow. Eduardo called an all-hands meeting for the fire station, first thing."

Tammy rolled her eyes. "You know, you don't have to wait. You could just go over to the other side of the office and introduce yourself."

"I'm sure he's getting plenty warm welcomes from all the other ladies, if he's what you say he is. I'd rather give the poor guy a chance to settle in before being ripped to pieces by that community group."

Just as she finished saying it, a man she'd never met before peeked into the opening of her cubicle. He looked tall—at least six feet. He wore his longish, dark hair back in a short ponytail, and sported a neatly trimmed mustache and beard. His grey button-up shirt and black pants fit him well, but the tie looked like it had been knotted by a teenager. A strand of disobedient hair escaped from the ponytail and fell over his eyes in a spiral. Even without necktie acumen, Hannah could tell that he had yet to be ripped to pieces by anyone or anything. He flashed a smile that could have seduced all 40 protesting residents. When he spoke, his voice was a pleasant tenor. "I hope for my sake they give me a shot at running before the carnage begins."

Tammy laughed loudly and stood up. "Hi, Danny—you settling in okay? Hannah Mercury, meet Danny Ayres, our newest crusading civil servant." Hannah felt like sinking into the ground, but instead she got up and offered her hand. "Hannah's the project manager for the new fire station."

Danny Ayres stood with an almost bewitched smile directed at Hannah. "Technically, I don't have the luck or stability of being a civil servant like you, but I'm excited to work with you nonetheless."

"Nice to meet you, Danny," said Hannah. "Look, I'm sorry for what I said about the community group…"

Danny's smile held strong. "Please don't be. I'm glad there's some-one around who'll give it to me straight. Trust me, the more I know about these folks, the better. My job stability will be based on results. Our work starts today, so there's no time to sing me lullabies before sending me into the lion's den."

Hannah laughed. "You seem rather confident you'll come out tri-umphant."

Danny winked. "I always do."

Hannah couldn't help but be charmed, despite herself. Lucky for her she had no interest in guys with long hair and big egos, and hadn't since she'd gazed dreamily at Michael Hutchence's image on the "Kick" album in 1988. Still, she recognized that a bit of good, ol' fashioned arrogance was probably exactly what they needed to get the project back on track. "Well, for all our sakes, I hope you do. Honestly, there's very little wiggle room for us to completely change the plans at this point. We're running way behind schedule, and even if we get approval to go out to bid within the next six months, we'll be lucky if we start construc-tion in time to retain the federal funding."

"I'd love to hear more about all the funding issues, and how they play into the project's timeline," said Danny—not ironically at all.

Hannah nodded. "Well, the best brain to pick on that is Connor Dalton. He's the project's finance coordinator."

Was that disappointment on his face? "Oh, great. Well—guess I'll stop by his workspace next."

"Two aisles down, second cubicle on the right." Hannah pointed him in the right direction.

Danny winked again. "Thanks—nice to meet you, Hannah. Tam-my—I've got my eye on you." Tammy giggled mischievously.

Hannah, eyes rolling, turned back to her friend once he was gone. "Really, Tammy—you're gonna fall for that?" She tried to keep her voice low enough so that no one else could hear.

"Oh, come on, Hannah—where's your sense of fun? He's just kidding around. I doubt he'd go for me anyway. Looks like he could manage to get any sort of model-type of his dreams." Shaking her head, Hannah took a final bite of her breakfast. "You should have talked to him about the financing—you know enough about it."

Hannah threw away the oatmeal cup. "Nope—let him deal with the expert on that. I have a transmittal to write."

*

Danny was only half-listening to Connor Dalton drone on about the project's financing. He needed to know enough to answer any questions that might come up during community meetings, but it wasn't like he needed all the down-and-dirty details. He let his mind wander to that gal, Tammy. She seemed like she would be a fun person to have in his corner, and didn't seem too stuck up to kid around. Now, that Hannah was another story. He had noted she was pretty cute—blond and petite, not really his type—but she seemed a little uptight. Still, it would help to have someone more interested in setting him straight than charming his pants off. And, from what he heard about this project, it was probably good that she let the uptight overshadow the cute—might make her more legit in the eyes of that community group that he had to shift. Anyway, his days of running around were over. He was determined to figure out a way to make Akie see how good they were together.

After he'd left Unchained that awful week, Akie had called to give her support. She hadn't offered to come over, but gave more of a general "I'm here if you need me" sort of speech, one that seemed the smallest bit non-committal.

And why should she commit to a guy that was out of a job? Danny had determined after hanging up with her that the most important move for him would be to re-establish himself, career-wise, and Akie would follow. There was no way he could be anything to her if he didn't even have the means to support himself.

He knew jobs in the music industry were scarce, and financially he couldn't be out of a job for more than a month, not unless he wanted to downgrade his life. Waiting for his dream job would do him no good. Lucky for him, there were a lot of other marketing jobs up for grabs. But when he saw the listing for this one, he knew it was the best quick solution: a stable government job, with health benefits and steady pay, hiring now. He needed Akie to see him as a provider, and this job was the perfect start.

He was pulled out of his musing by the words, "Do you want to get a drink and maybe some lunch? Then I can tell you all the *real* challenges of working in this place." It was the first English he'd heard Connor speak.

"Is that okay?"

Connor shrugged. "There are few rules that govern what we do when we are off duty."

Danny laughed. "Sounds good. Lead the way."

*

Danny was glad he walked into the meeting having had a candid conversation with Connor the day before. It helped him to understand all the little political bits that started coming into play almost as soon as the meeting began.

Eduardo, the Division Director, stood up. "Okay, everyone, thanks for being here. I trust you've all met Danny Ayres, our new P.R. Specialist. Danny's going to make sure we get as little pushback as possible from the neighborhood council."

A tough-looking woman he met briefly yesterday—Hortencia or something—started to speak. "I'm sorry, how are we doing our job if all we do is try to get around the community? This fire station is for their benefit, true, but I think the more we take their concerns seriously the less political backlash we'll get in the end."

Hannah shook her head. "Hortencia, the clock is already ticking on this thing. We don't have time to re-start the project. The federal funding stipulates when construction needs to begin, and by my calendar we are already in seriously hot water."

"Hannah, you know I respect your opinion and I know you are looking at this purely from a project management point-of-view. But if we keep on going like we've solved all the problems once this thing is steamrolled through Council, the hot water will just be dammed up by a very unstable barrier. We as a City will still have to answer to the people. I cannot believe that there isn't the option to request an extension from the Feds. Connor," she directed her attention to the finance coordinator, who had just walked in. "Can't extensions be granted by the funding agency?"

Connor sat down hesitantly in the only seat left open, the one next to Hannah. "Sorry I'm late, Eduardo. Hortencia, to answer your question, yes. I've already briefed Hannah on that option." He kept looking towards Hortencia when he mentioned Hannah, with not so much as a glance in her direction.

Hannah shifted uncomfortably in her seat. Danny noticed that her face had become flushed and that a frown had creased her previously cool and expressionless forehead. "I—yes, Connor, you have. And I think the conversation that followed was that there are no guarantees that an extension will be granted, just because we request one." She said this glancing in his general direction the whole time, but at no point did their eyes meet. He knew Hannah seemed uptight, but she hadn't seemed anti-social to him.

What's going on there?

But instead of voicing that thought, he decided to help out. "You know, if I do my job right, we'll have real community buy-in on this thing, not just lip service, and at the same time be able to check off our list of requirements from the Feds. I have done a lot more with a whole lot less in much less time than six months." Hannah smiled gratefully at him, Hortencia seemed less riled, and Connor nodded. Win, win, win.

The meeting progressed efficiently for the next hour, and then Danny spent the rest of the morning looking at background documentation and constituent's public statement cards about the project. Before he knew it, it was lunchtime. He'd seen a sushi place that he wanted to try a few blocks away, and headed over there to check it out.

The sushi place was having one crazy rush hour. He put in his order at the register, and then glanced around for a seat in the small dining area. No open tables, but one table for two that was occupied by only one attractive little blond: Hannah. She had her phone in one hand and a pair of chopsticks in the other, looming over a plateful of salmon sushi, and hadn't even noticed Danny walk in. He thought about something Connor had said about her yesterday: "I watch my step around that one." At the time he thought it had to do with her no-nonsense business style, and didn't pursue it any further, but judging from that interaction between those two during the meeting this morning, Danny wondered if there wasn't some more interesting story. Besides, Hannah seemed nice enough. Maybe Connor just didn't gel with her. He decided to take the risk and join her.

"Mind if I hijack half of your table?"

She looked up from her phone, and registered a smile when she realized who it was. "Not at all—the place gets busy, and I've done my share of hijacking in the past."

"Cool." He settled across from her. "Busy little place."

"Yeah, well, it's the closest sushi to our office, and the lunch specials aren't bad at all." She tucked her phone into a side pocket on her purse.

"Of course, I always just get my four orders of salmon sushi, but the Deluxe is a pretty good deal."

"Yep, that's what I got. You come here a lot, then?"

"It's in my regular rotation. I try to get around to all the little places within a half-mile radius, but truth be told there aren't that many, and I'm getting a little tired of them."

"Ever think of driving out somewhere else?"

Hannah shrugged. "I take public transit, so I'm pretty much dependent on someone else to drive me out to interesting places. The DASH from here takes a little long when you only get a half-hour."

"Management's pretty flexible, though, right? I drive. If you're willing to take more than a half-hour every once in a while, I'd be happy to try out places beyond the neighborhood here. It's my first time working in Downtown L.A., and I'm looking to make the most of it. Maybe we could get a little group together or something."

"That might be fun," Hannah said in that vague way sweet girls blew off men they didn't want to deal with.

"And just in case you're worried that I'm trying to hit on you," Hannah burst into laughter at this, "I promise you it's just lunch I'm after. Not looking to complicate my love life any more than it already is."

Hannah seemed truly at ease with these words. "I believe you. Sure, I'll take you on a weekly tour of some must-hit places in Downtown."

It turned out that a few other people were getting tired of the neighborhood's offerings for lunch. That first Thursday, five of them, including Hannah, Tammy, Elena from Accounting, and Eduardo's assistant Dominic, piled into Danny's crossover SUV to trek over to Philippe's in Chinatown. A heated debate ensued about whether Cole's on Main offered the better French Dip, so they all decided to settle the matter two Thursdays later, after payday. The group split 3:2 once they had a chance to sample the latter, with Philippe's barely squeaking by with the victory. Then someone mentioned burgers, and everyone realized that the score needed to be settled on whether Umami or The Counter had the edge. After both those had been tested, someone else threw The Escondite into the ring. That week, everyone agreed they'd found their burger heaven. When they got back to the office, Hannah lingered in Danny's workspace for a bit.

"Do I have anything stuck in my teeth?" She bared her teeth to Danny.

"Nope, you're clean."

"So are you. Your teeth, I mean. The rest of you—I can't account for." Hannah imitated Danny's trademark wink.

"Don't hate the playa."

Hannah laughed. "So I guess from everyone's plans we'll have to put our Thursday explorations on hiatus. June's vacation time."

"We can always go rogue as we see fit—don't always gotta plan things out so far."

"A week's far?" Hannah asked, eyebrows raised. Danny shrugged. "I guess we don't."

"We can always invite different people, too. Like Connor—I was talking to him the other day about Langers…" Hannah was already shaking her head furiously. "What?"

"Not a good idea, Danny." She spoke low, like she was afraid someone else would hear.

He lowered his voice, as well. "You two don't get along, do you?"

Hannah took in a deep breath, then exhaled. "We used to."

"Oh. Well—then maybe all you need is just a chance to re-connect."

"I don't think that's going to happen over lunch, Danny." She leaned over and spoke almost so low he had to read her lips. "My marital problems started with Connor."

Understanding flooded into Danny's brain. There were a lot of things going on at that moment. First was surprise—Hannah never struck him at all as the kind of woman who'd let herself get caught up in relationship drama, though he knew from their conversations at lunch that she was recently separated from her husband, and that the two still lived in the same house with their kids. Second was admiration—after all, Connor was a younger man. Third was determination—if things weren't gonna work out with her husband, he thought she deserved a chance at happiness. Good people should be with the ones they loved. He thought sadly of Akie. And an idea suddenly flashed to his brain. "Maybe it won't happen over lunch—but what about happy hour?"

Hannah looked doubtful. "The other finance folks are always going out after work. But I have never once been invited. I guess they think I can't, what with the whole mom thing. Nobody realizes that I do get a night out every once in a while."

Danny waved his hand in dismissal. "So we plan our own happy hour. We invite the people nobody else ever invites and make a whole fun night outta it."

Hannah smiled. "The renegades?"

"The rejects. Reject happy hour."

Hannah allowed a burst of laughter to come forth. "Reject, huh? I like the sound of that. It sure describes my status in Connor's eyes."

"Not once we're done. We'll invite him, too."

"He won't come. He never shows if he knows I'm going to be there. I used to try it with lunch, before you came in with your crossover SUV and saved the day."

Danny groaned. "Don't call it a crossover. It sounds so much less cool when you say that."

"Nothing wrong with utilitarian."

"And there's nothin' wrong with trying. I'm gonna do my best to get Connor there." Hannah shot him another dubious glance. "Come on, you never know with these things. And if he doesn't show—well, we had fun trying. Now, why don't you and Tammy put your heads together and think of all the rejects we're gonna invite?"

"Definitely the regular lunch group. I'll ask Tammy who else might enjoy a night out—there are a lot of people in this office who don't drink, so I want to make sure not to ask the wrong people, either."

"You're not gonna ask anybody. You'll tell me who to invite, and I'm gonna put the word out myself, make sure this looks like it's coming from me and only me."

"Ah-ha," Hannah mused, nodding her head, "Controlling the message from the start? That's my P.R. buddy at his finest."

"It's what I do. Now, are there any sorta low-key, casual bars around here?"

Hannah laughed again. "Oh, Danny, you are so asking the wrong person. The only bar I ever went to in recent years was the one I went to with Connor. And I don't ever want to go back."

Danny looked at her questioningly. "You must have done your share of partying before the whole married mom thing?"

Hannah shook her head. "I was every parent's dream my whole life, even when my parents stopped needing to know my after-hours movements."

"You mean you've never been on a bar-hop?"

"I haven't been to that many bars, much less a bar-hop. How do you do that, you just go to as many bars as you can in one night?"

"Hannah Mercury, you are gonna find that out for yourself. It is my job as your drinking guru to indoctrinate you into the whole drinking sub-culture, one bar at a time. You have waited way too long and been too good."

"Not that good."

"Too good. Let's run a little bad into those veins. Now, what day works for you?"

"*That* I will have to decide with my husband. Don't know really how I'm supposed to approach it."

"You approach it like you're having a night out with some friends, which you are. You don't have to show him a guest list."

"True. I'll touch bases with him tonight and let you know tomorrow." Hannah got up to go, but stopped as she got to the opening of his cubicle. She offered a big grin to Danny. "Thanks, Danny. You're an awesome friend."

"I just like to hang with fun people."

Hannah smiled again, then walked toward her own workspace.

*

Danny thought a lot that evening of Hannah, of her rejection with Connor, and his newfound quest to help her find happiness. It had been three months now since he'd proposed and had experienced a heavy dose of his own rejection. He'd not seen much of Akie since. She had apparently been asked to take over all his old accounts, and had been traveling pretty extensively as a result. And if he was honest with himself, he envied her that life, which up until recently he had lived himself. It was as if winning Hannah a little bit of her dream would give him the confidence to make real his own; like playing *her* way back into Connor's heart would prove that he could play Akie back into *his*.

He looked down at his watch. It was 6:30, and they were meeting for band practice in an hour. Danny and Gavin had agreed that, although Gavin had the voice, Danny didn't quite have the skill to be the lead guitar, and they had enlisted Gavin's friend Mark, who once had a band that hit it big enough to be played on all the college stations. Mark knew a guy through his brother-in-law that was a pretty decent drummer, and they brought him on board a month ago. Danny rounded them out on bass. Danny had offered some of his old Exquisite Corpse stuff, but Gavin wanted to go with stuff that wasn't quite so heady, and had been working with Mark to come up with a new sound that would sell. They'd rented a space in Silverlake and had been pretty diligent with practice twice a week. Danny always made sure to get to work a little late on those days, so he could just hang out after hours and work on the fire station stuff without interruption. It actually worked out pretty well, when his mind wasn't full of thoughts on how to get Akie back. He decided to try giving her a call, picked up his cell phone, and dialed her number.

"Hello?" Her voice sounded sexy and pleasant, even when she was just answering the phone.

"Hey."

"Danny? Is that you?"

"Yeah, it's me. I was thinking it's been awhile since we got together." Might as well cut to the chase.

"Oh, yeah, it totally has. I just got back into town two days ago."

"Unchained's got you running around everywhere, don't they?"

"It's a living. What about you, how's that new job going?"

"Not so new anymore. I've been there two months now."

There was a pause. "Geez, has it really been that long? It feels like I just saw you a few weeks ago."

"Doesn't feel like that to me. You wanna get together for lunch or something next week?" Danny realized then that she may not be free to accept his offer as a date—he wouldn't be surprised if she was dating a few guys. "That is, if you have the time to meet with an old friend."

He could almost hear her smile over the phone. "Always. We could meet halfway, East Hollywood or something."

"I don't mind coming over there."

"Grub? Thursday at Noon?"

"Sounds like a plan. I'll pick you up." Danny didn't know the last time he'd looked so forward to eating lunch.

*

Danny saw the little popup box come up on his chat: "Hannah: The Peruvian place is open!"

Danny typed his reply: "The one near the Macy's?"

"Hannah: That's the one. Tammy and I are gonna check it out. Game?"

Too bad. He always had fun with Hannah. "Sorry, can't. Plans."

"Hannah: No worries. This is why I plan a week out. LOL. See you later."

He left early so he could get to Akie before their planned meeting time. Before heading out, he made sure his teeth were brushed and his hair out of the ponytail. He looked in the mirror: clean shave around his beard holding up okay, no zits. He was ready to spend time with the girl of his dreams.

When Akie came out of Unchained's headquarters, she looked like that dream come true, in a snug-fitting red skirt and white short-sleeved blouse. She opened his passenger door and gave him a quick hug before settling into the seat. "Thanks for picking me up."

"No problem. How are things?"

"Good. I'm hungry, though."

"Well, you sure picked the right spot." They continued the small talk during the drive to Grub, during the walk up to request a table, and after they were seated. It seemed like she was trying to think of unimportant things to say as filler, like there was something she was waiting to say at the right time. After they ordered, she drew in her breath.

"I've got some good news. Unchained is promoting me!"

"What? Akie, that's great news! What'll they have you doing?"

"Well, that's even bigger news. They want me to clean up the Tokyo office for the next 6 months." At that moment, the waitress brought their drinks. Akie took a sip of her mimosa.

Danny felt like he'd been punched in the gut. He looked down at his coffee. "Wow, Akie. That's a big change. You just moved from there."

"Yeah, but it's a good chance for me to really make my mark with the company."

"But you still have things you can do here." He was trying to think of things to say that wouldn't sound like a desperate attempt to beg that she stay.

"They think I can do better things there." She was swigging that mimosa pretty quickly.

"You've already made your decision, huh?"

She polished off the mimosa. "There's really no other decision to make. I took this job knowing it would be a mobile one. I like that about this job. No offense, I know you like your new stable job, but I think I'd get bored reporting to the same office and seeing the same people every day for weeks on end, with no break."

"When do you leave?"

"Next month."

Danny didn't think about what he said next. There was no time. "Take the rest of the day off with me. I promise I'll make it worth your while." The food arrived, and Akie looked at Danny with somewhat glazed eyes.

"We can't do that."

"Why not? I know your bosses give you free reign, and I can just say I got some food poisoning or something."

Akie smiled. "Okay, Danny. Let's play hooky."

They ate quickly, paying the bill and getting to the car in 10 minutes. Once they were settled in the car, Danny put his hand on Akie's knee.

"Where to?" He slid his fingers under her hemline, and slowly moved his hand up her inner thigh, until it was just outside of her panty line. He rubbed slowly, letting his fingertips brush the outside of her crotch. Her skin was as soft as he remembered, and her panties felt silky and sexy.

"My place is about 10 minutes north of here," she said with labored breathing.

"Lead the way."

She gave him breathless directions to her place as he played around the line of her panties with his free hand. When he looked over at a light, she had her eyes closed and her face was flushed. She reached her hand over to his jeans, and brushed her fingers against the hardness there.

When they got to her apartment building, they quickly found parking and got out of the car. She fumbled around with her purse, and Danny could tell that she had gotten tipsy off the one mimosa. She finally found her keys, and they walked in and up a flight of stairs until they reached a door that she started to unlock. "It's a mess."

"I don't care." Once the door was open and they were both inside, Danny grabbed her and pressed her against the door. He pulled up her skirt and started rubbing more vigorously against her crotch with one hand, pulling down her panties while unbuttoning his jeans with the other. As soon as he had the buttons undone and pushed his pants down with his briefs, he rubbed himself against her soft pussy. "Feel how much I want you?" He got down on his knees and plunged his tongue into that softness, kissing her outer lips with his mouth while he tasted the inside of her. He wanted her all. He wanted her to want him. He stood up and kissed her mouth deeply. "I want you to feel how much I need you." He put his hands on her shoulders and pushed her down.

She brushed her lips against him, and then looked up, unbuttoning her top and allowing her breasts to pop out. "Are you ready for me?"

"I've been ready," he said. He shrugged out of his pants and got on his knees while he turned her around. She put her hands on the floor, and he guided his cock into her. She was tight, but a little wet from his work. He gave a few slower thrusts, and then let himself move with reckless abandon. As he jackhammered into her, he grabbed her from behind, holding her across her shoulders with his left arm while he fondled her overflowing breasts with his right. He brushed the left arm over her tits, so he could tickle her clit while he continued to thrust. She grunted with each pound.

"Danny," she managed to say between grunts, "We forgot the condom again."

"Oh, yeah," he said. He withdrew long enough to grab his abandoned jeans and find the condom he had quickly pushed into the pocket this morning. Ripping the package open, his slid it onto himself, then thrust back in and continued his urgent hammering. She groaned a little. As he felt himself close, he went even faster. "I'm gonna fuck you so hard and so good you will never want to go to Tokyo again." Her grunting was synced with his thrusting, and he felt himself begin to come. He gave one last, hard thrust, and he was done.

He released her from his grip, and she got back down on her hands, panting. He stayed on his knees for a while, still inside of her, and wiped the sweat off his brow. He broke away from her, collapsing on the floor. He closed his eyes, enjoying the quiet and the cool air. "Nice place you have here."

She laughed briefly. "Wow."

"Give me a minute and we can go again."

She lifted herself up, pulling at her underwear. "I gotta go use the bathroom—you want me to get rid of that for you?" She indicated the used condom still clinging to his member. He smiled lazily and peeled it off, handing it to her. She left for a few minutes, while Danny let himself nod off a little. He roused when he heard her come back, and saw that her skirt was back in place, her blouse buttoned, and her hair neatened.

"Going somewhere?"

"Danny, I really have to get back to work. I'm sorry, I know you wanted to take the day, but there are just way too many things to do."

He laid there in disbelief, flaccid member still resting on his leg. "It can't wait?"

"No, Danny, it really can't. I'm sorry."

Although he was thinking *What the fuck*, he got up and said, "All right. I understand." He pulled his pants on hastily, tucked in his shirt and patted his hair down. "I'll get you back to your office." He walked out into the hallway, and as she locked the door he looked down at his watch. He'd been gone for almost two hours. Hopefully nobody noticed.

There was no focusing when he got back to his computer at work. He just couldn't understand what was going on with Akie. It was like she was afraid to get too close to him, so she sabotaged every moment they had together. Was she that focused on advancing her career? He supposed he really didn't blame her, but he couldn't help thinking that something else might be going on.

"How was your lunch?"

Danny looked up and saw Hannah. "Hey…it was cool."

She sat down in his guest chair. "You were a million miles away there."

"Yeah, I have a friend I'm kinda worried about. I think she's sabotaging herself."

Hannah looked at him sympathetically. "That's rough. Difficult to know what to do when someone you care about is going down a path you can't support." He nodded absentmindedly. "That tends to be my cue to back off."

He looked up. It sounded like something he would have said once. "Yeah, I guess."

"No better place to back into than a bar." She raised an eyebrow.

He laughed—*that* definitely was something he would have said. "Good point. You ready for next week?"

"I'm actually really excited!" Her eyes widened in surprise when she said it.

He thought to himself how cute she was. "Good! I got you and Tammy in, Dominic's in, Elena thinks she can stop by for an hour."

Hannah looked over to the aisle, and then looked at him and mouthed, "Connor?"

He lowered his voice. "Not yet, but I'm working on it. And I was thinking of inviting my bandmate, Mark. My friend Gav just got married, so he's not into spending the night with anyone except his wife."

"Sounds like a good guy. Hey, I didn't know you were in a band?"

"Oh, yeah—I never said anything?"

"*No!* What kind of music do you guys play?"

"Sorta punk pop influence. Not really my kinda music."

"What instrument do you play?"

"Bass."

"So you don't write the music?"

"Not for this one."

"So you have written music?"

"I have." He leaned over into his desk drawer, and dug through some CDs he had in there. "First thing you gotta know about musicians is that we always carry our own music with us. Here," he said, handing her one labeled, *Exquisite Corpse.*

She grabbed it. "Can I take this home with me?"

"Of course! I wrote and produced it myself. I was really proud of that."

"Why'd you stop?"

"It was never really commercially viable. Not even my new band wants to play any of it."

"Well, *I* can't wait to play it. Listen to it." She hugged it to her body. "You are just full of surprises, Danny Ayres."

He smiled. "What can I say? I'm a man of many talents."

"I'll bet you are." She raised her eyebrows, but then burst into laughter.

Track 3

Hannah appraised her image in the mirror of the office bathroom. She hoped she looked okay. She'd gotten up extra early that morning to pick out something that was casual enough for the low-key bar they would be visiting, work-appropriate, cute enough so that she felt on-par with the doubtless plentiful young people that would be in the place, and comfortable enough so that she could wear sneakers with it. The sneakers were a must—she figured if they were doing a bar-hop they would be walking, and no use wearing a cute pair of heels when she'd just be hating them later in the night for the blisters they would cause. She went with a semi-casual coral-colored cotton weave dress with a scoop neck, ruffled bottom, and ruffled cap sleeves (way shorter than she was used to wearing), a fitted denim blazer, and her somewhat beat-up red sneakers. She kept pumps in her desk at work, so she could wear those in the office and change back into the sneakers when it was time to cut out. Her 8-year old had commented on how pretty she looked, so how bad could it be? Looking over her image again now that she'd been in the outfit all day, she decided it was a good choice: minimum wrinkling; and she had a fun, young look to her.

Not that she was old. After all, she was still in her mid-thirties (thirty-six was still mid, right?) and she was always told she looked younger. She'd recently cut her blond hair to just at her chin, and it really brightened her face. Her boobs were small, but this dress played up what she had as much as possible, just in case Connor did decide to join them. Not that he wasn't already fully aware of the size of her boobs. She remembered how she'd joked that it was mostly padding, and how as he'd begun to fondle them he looked deep into her eyes and said he didn't care. She felt her heart flutter, and reminded herself not to get too worked up. Disappointment was standard when dealing with him.

She turned away from her image and left the bathroom. Anyways, it would be a fun time without Connor, too. Maybe more fun. He did have a sort of chip-on-his-shoulder attitude when he was around other people. So totally different from Danny.

Danny. She smiled every time she thought of him. She'd never expected when she met him that first day how close they would become so quickly. He was just such an open person—everyone in the office liked him. He had a way of putting a person completely at ease within minutes of meeting. She had seen this in action the past few months as they worked together to canvas the community groups in the neighborhood of the new fire station. He could strike up a conversation with anyone, from an apathetic teen to a suspicious elderly lady, and have them laughing and joking at the end of the conversation. In a very short time, they were gaining momentum for fast-tracking approval of the site. They'd explained to the youth center how essential the station was for quick responses to the sorts of emergencies that would no doubt occur because "kids will be kids". They'd appealed to the senior center and adult day-care how, even though the closest fire station now was less than 5 miles away, in rush-hour valley traffic that could mean the difference between life and death for a senior in dire need. They'd met with local businesses, who of course had plenty to lose if response time was impacted by distance. They were methodically bringing stakeholders on board, so that when the time came to face the greatest challenger, the neighborhood council, they would have a number of constituents in their corner.

Hannah swung by Danny's cubicle on the way to her own. She hadn't seen him all day, and knew that he'd been running against a tight deadline to prepare a presentation for updating management on his progress. When she peeked in, he was entering data into a report. "Hey," she said casually.

He turned around as he said, "Hey." Then when he saw her, a big smile spread over his face. "You look cute."

Hannah blushed, shrugging her shoulders. "Thank you. I wasn't sure what to wear, so I hope this is okay."

"You better be ready to fend off leering men, missy."

Hannah laughed. "Hardly. I just hope I can hold my liquor long enough to get to the second bar."

"All about pacing. I'll be there to guide you through it." He winked.

"Well, I've got all evening to learn. My husband was okay with me being out past dinnertime. What time do you want to head over?"

He looked back at his computer. "I gotta get this report finished. You may need to head over without me and grab a good spot."

"Okay! Don't work too late."

"No worries there. I'll be right behind you."

When Tammy and Hannah got to the Library Bar, there were already a good number of people. A really cool space with sofas and crammed bookshelves had "Reserved" signs on the coffee tables, so they couldn't settle there. They went over to the end of the bar and looked up at the drink boards. "The cosmo looks good. Happy hour special."

Tammy settled into a bar stool. "I think I'm gonna get something on tap."

Hannah raised an eyebrow. "Once you go down the beer road, forever may it cloud your destiny. I haven't done much drinking, but that much I do know."

"Yeah, but it'll also fill me up a little. You never eat much at these things. We'll order some sliders and fries to pad it a bit."

"Good point. I'll get an Arrogant Bastard, in honor of Danny for organizing this thing."

"Haha! Good choice!"

She was almost halfway done and feeling good by the time Danny walked in with a guy she'd never met who had short-cropped black hair and a serious demeanor. She held up the bottle so they could see. "In your honor."

Danny smiled. "Good one!" They hugged. He seemed taller when she didn't have her heels on, and smelled amazing. Danny indicated his friend. "I want you guys to meet Mark, lead guitarist for our yet-to-be-named band."

"Nice to know you, Mark," said Hannah.

"Good to meet you," said Tammy.

"Likewise." He looked over at Danny. "What're you getting?"

Danny appraised the drink board. "The stout looks good."

Mark gave their order to the bartender, and they all settled at the end of the bar with their drinks. Danny came up next to Hannah, putting his arm around her and leaning over as he whispered in her ear. "I couldn't get Connor to come."

She immediately hid her disappointment, taking a swig of her beer. "That's okay," she said into his ear. "I'm here to be with you guys, not him." She spontaneously kissed him on his cheek. He looked down at her and smiled, and as he did Elena, Dominic, and Eduardo walked in. Hannah saw them first. "Hey!" She quickly went over and hugged each one of them. "Eduardo, I didn't know you would be here."

He laughed. "Hope having the boss here doesn't put a damper on the festivities."

"You're not *my* boss," said Elena, putting her hand on his shoulder. They both burst into laughter. Introductions were passed all around.

"Why don't we settle over there?" asked Eduardo, indicating the library area.

"Reserved," said Tammy, shrugging.

Eduardo went up to the bar and said something to the bartender. He turned back around to the rest of the group. "Not reserved 'til 9:30. He said we can sit here until then."

They settled onto the couches. Hannah put one foot on the coffee table, crossing the other over it. Danny took a seat next to her. He reached his arm out to touch her sneaker, letting his finger stop at her ankle. It made her tingle.

She laughed. "I know, it doesn't really go with the rest of the outfit. Not the best look, but it's good for walking. We *are* gonna do a bar hop, tonight, right?"

He squeezed her ankle and settled back next to her. "That's what I promised."

She leaned back, resting her shoulder against his. They gazed contentedly at each other for a few seconds. She thought about how sad he looked last week. "Are you feeling better this week? You know, about your friend?"

He shrugged. "Not much I can do about it, I guess."

"Do you mind me asking what happened?"

He looked down. "She's sorta the girl I'm crazy about. I thought things were going pretty well, but then she told me that she's moving out of the country."

"What?!"

"Yeah, she got a really good opportunity with her job. She's in the music business like I was. It's a smart move, career-wise, but..." He trailed off.

Hannah understood. "You want her to be with you."

He kept his eyes focused on his feet. "It's selfish, I know."

Hannah put her hand on his arm. "Loving someone can be a little selfish. But if you want to be with her, you have to let her know how much she means to you. You can't let her pass up a chance at happiness just because you don't want to sound too selfish."

He glanced over at her, mouth upturned slightly. "I don't really know what to say."

She leaned her head back against the couch. "Just say what you feel." He nodded. She didn't know why, but she felt moved by this new knowledge. It reminded her of how she felt with Connor—wanting to be with someone that just wants to stay away. And she suddenly felt passionate about helping Danny reach out to this girl he wanted. Why shouldn't someone have a happy ending? "Is there anything I can do to help?"

Danny grabbed her shoe and settled it onto his lap. "Have another drink with me."

She laughed, and pushed away his lap with her foot. "Gladly! Go get me a porter."

That sadness that had registered on his face just a few minutes ago was gone, and his eyes twinkled mischievously. "Yes, ma'am. But don't pound this one, okay? Pacing, remember?"

"Yes, sir!"

They stayed for another hour, Hannah nursing her drink. Dominic's sister showed up. Elena decided she had to get home. Then Eduardo mentioned a dive bar he knew down Broadway, and the remaining group headed out towards their new destination. When they got there, however, the place was closed down for a film shoot. Somebody mentioned another place, not too far on 8th. Hannah was grateful for her comfortable shoes. Their third destination was dark, low key, not too crowded, and only very slightly divey. She felt completely at ease and slightly drunk. She looked at her watch. She couldn't take advantage of her husband for too much longer.

Danny walked up to her, placing his arm around her waist and squeezing tight. It kind of felt like manhandling to Hannah, but at the same time felt really good. "What'll you have?"

She eased her arm around him and squeezed back. "Water."

"Folding already?"

"Yeah, I gotta drive in an hour, so I better spend it sobering up."

"Good idea." He went to go get drinks while the others settled into a large, circular booth. Hannah ended up between Mark and Eduardo, and they had a good conversation about dive bars in the area. She was glad to be out tonight; it had afforded her a chance to get to know people she wouldn't otherwise have gotten to know, and to spend after-hours time with Danny and Tammy. This was a nice place to wind down, too. Its brick walls lent an intimate air, and a couple of arcade games added some fun.

When Danny got back, he handed Hannah the water and settled into the booth across from her. "So how are you liking your first bar hop?"

Mark looked down at her. "This is your first? I didn't know you were a virgin." Everyone burst into laughter.

Hannah felt herself blush. "Well, I want to thank you all for being gentle, and making a girl's first time something to remember. Now, when do we do it again?"

"Once is not enough," said Tammy suggestively.

Eduardo got out his phone, apparently to look at his calendar. "How about two weeks from today?"

"That would be my birthday," said Danny.

Hannah gave a nod. "Oh, well then you probably have plans."

"Nope."

"Doesn't your family do anything for you, like a cake or something?" Tammy asked.

"They all live outta state. I usually lay pretty low on my birthday."

Hannah gave a toast with her water glass. "Well, you won't this birthday. We'll take you out again and show you how to celebrate!"

Everyone else raised their glasses. Danny laughed. "Creeping into my late thirties doesn't seem like something to celebrate."

Hannah shook her head. "Every year is something to celebrate, and pretty soon I'll be right there with you. So let's walk into it together." She leaned over and held her glass in front of him.

He gave a look that pierced right into her. "To walking together," and he tapped her glass. She felt another tingle in her stomach—but the moment was interrupted by a new conversation about where they should go. It looked like Hannah's second time would be even more special than the first.

*

The long weekend had been a welcome break, especially since Hannah had been ever so slightly hung over. She had been sluggish all weekend, but her husband had been a sweetheart and really helped keep the kids distracted. She was so surprised at how supportive he had been, considering he was gaining nothing by letting her go out with her friends. She resolved to ask him if he wanted a night out with his friends, too, just to be fair.

She found herself thinking a lot about Danny that weekend, hoping that everything worked out for the best where that girl he liked was concerned. He tried to act so cocky, but she could tell there was a deep vulnerability there that he kept hidden, and she'd seen a little of that during their happy hour. It intrigued her, and made her want to do everything she could to help him out. Or, if she couldn't help him, to make him feel better. Maybe this birthday happy hour would be exactly the thing that would bring up his spirits, and give him the confidence he needed to fight for the girl that he loved.

*

Danny paused before knocking on Akie's door. He'd just found out that today—his birthday—was her last day in town. It was shitty, the way he'd found out. He'd run into Ned at a convenience store at lunch, and had to endure an uncomfortable conversation before Ned mentioned that the previous week had been Akie's last in the Hollywood office, and she had been spending the current week packing. Danny didn't understand why Akie hadn't told him. He'd sort of kept his distance for the last few weeks, giving her some space and time to miss him, thinking he'd call her before she left. She *had* said she was leaving in July, but he had no idea it was so soon in July. So he decided to make one last-ditch effort and stop by her place, unexpected, before going back to the office. He felt sort of humiliated having to do it, but he'd rather be humiliated for a few minutes if it meant the possibility of her reconsidering her future with him. He knocked.

Akie answered the door, her long hair pulled back in a looped ponytail. She had a tight-fitting t-shirt and some short cutoffs on, and her feet were bare. She looked amazing. Her eyebrows raised when she saw him. "Danny—I didn't know you were stopping by!"

"Neither did I, 'til I ran into Ned just now and found out you were leaving tomorrow. Why didn't you say anything?"

Akie looked around into the hallway, and looked up at Danny. "Why don't you come in for a sec, Danny?" She opened the door wider so that he could walk in, and closed the door behind him. He looked down at the floor where they'd made love only a few weeks ago. Then he looked up and noticed that her whole place was pretty much in boxes, and there were bags of trash scattered around the room. Akie closed the door behind him, and then turned his way. "Look, I didn't really know if I should contact you or not."

"Why wouldn't you know?"

Akie put her hands on her hips, and looked down. "I don't know, Danny. Our relationship has just been really weird for me."

"We're dating—what's so weird about that?"

"We were dating, Danny, until you proposed and I decided that I'd better back way the fuck off. You—you just sort of dived right into assuming that we were serious, when I really just thought we were casually dating."

Danny shook his head. "I'm sorry if that freaked you out, Akie. I was being impulsive, something I don't do that often when it comes to women. I just thought you were so amazing, and worried about you with all the layoffs...Obviously, I should have been worrying about myself."

Akie nodded. "I know, Danny, and you were really cool about keeping a comfortable distance when you left Unchained. I really appreciated that. It's why I agreed to have lunch with you. But then when we met, and I drank that mimosa...I don't know. I was just feeling so careless at the moment, and when you started messing around I thought, why not? But it just—it just didn't feel right once we got back here."

"What do you mean it didn't feel right? We had sex, what's wrong with that?"

Akie chortled. "That wasn't sex, Danny—that was fucking—hardcore, down and dirty fucking. And I have never let that happen with someone I considered an ex. And then you said something that really made me think it had been a wrong move. Something about fucking me so hard and so good that I'd never want to go back to Tokyo."

"That was just dirty talk, heat-of-the-moment type stuff. I didn't mean to offend you."

Akie put her hand up. "It didn't offend me, Danny. I knew we were fucking. I wanted to fuck. I just didn't realize the stakes you had placed on it. I think for you it was like you were trying to win me over or something. And that's why I just wanted to get away from the situation."

"So you just decide to cut out without a word or a goodbye?" Danny didn't know what he felt, but if he didn't know better it could have the sense of feeling somewhat used.

"I wasn't thinking, Danny—I'm sorry. And then time just really went into turbo-mode, what with settling things at the office and getting a sub-lessee here. I *just* found a place in Tokyo yesterday—I thought I'd be living out of a hotel. I hope you know you matter to me, but really I have just been trying to keep my head on straight and keep this whole move from totally spinning out of control."

A flood of sympathy suddenly hit Danny, and he thought how tough it must be for her, having to just up and leave when she thought she'd be in the States for a while. "I know, Akie. Sorry to come bursting in here like a jilted lover or something. Not usually my style at all."

Akie smiled. "Danny…I hope you know that I really want to stay friends with you. I mean, my stint in Tokyo should be only 6 months. So it's not like it's forever. And I'd really like a friend to come back to."

Danny opened his arms to her. "Oh, Akie—of course you have a friend." She moved into his arms, and they embraced. He could feel her breasts against his torso, and could feel from the hardness of her nipples that she wasn't wearing a bra. It got him excited. He clutched at her back to keep her pressed to him, and moved one hand down to cup her ass. He let his lips brush over hers, but she backed away from the embrace before they could kiss. He tried to change the mood by saying something impulsive. "Hey, you wanna have dinner your last night? I got a thing planned, but I'll bow out of it if you want."

"That's sweet, Danny, but I'm planning on going over to my mom's for dinner. She's gonna cook my favorite meal, and she's sort of inviting all the aunties and cousins, so…" She looked at him like she hoped he'd understand.

"No worries, completely cool. I just wanted to make sure you had someone to eat with." He moved toward the door.

Akie followed. "Thanks for stopping by, Danny. I'm glad we could put things right between us before I left." She opened the door.

Danny walked out. "See you in six months—be sure to text me your new number over there, okay?" He turned around to face her.

"I will. Goodbye, Danny." She waved, and then closed the door. Danny stood in the hallway for a few seconds, shook his head, and then made to get back to the office.

*

They decided to take the underground red line to the Tiki Ti, which was their destination for Danny's birthday. A few of them had been and were eager to try it again. Those that hadn't been had heard about it, and knew they were in for a treat.

They had already started by the time they walked off of the subway at Vermont and Sunset, having grabbed some snacks and a starter drink at a place nearer to their office. Hannah could feel the whiskey sour singing through her veins, and she was happy, even as Danny leaned over to her as they were walking and said, "I dunno if I can get Connor here tonight…he says he *may* try to join us in a little bit. He had some stuff to wrap up at the office."

Hannah shrugged. "I doubt he'll end up showing. I told you: he never goes if I'm there."

There were only a few scattered regulars at the Tiki Ti, and though the place was tiny, grabbing a table with plenty chairs was not a problem. Tammy and Hannah sat on one side; Elena and Danny sat on the other.

Dominic walked in soon after with his sister and they grabbed a few barstools next to the table. It was a cozy little cocoon of friends.

Danny looked down at his phone. "It's Connor..." He laughed at whatever was texted, and typed something back.

"Is he coming?" asked Dominic.

"He's thinking he'll be over in about a half hour," said Danny, still typing. "He just texted some hip hop lyrics. I'm throwing some Tone Loc his way."

A barrage of 1990s hip hop tag lines was thrown around at that moment, but Hannah was only half-listening. She excused herself to go to the ladies' room. The thought that Connor might actually make it tonight put butterflies in her stomach. She looked in the mirror and decided she needed more lipstick. She told herself it was *not* for Connor's sake. And she knew that even she didn't buy that for one second.

When she got back, a second gargantuan drink had been placed in Hannah's spot. She was still buzzed from the Blue Hawaiian that she had just sucked down, which had been as big as two drinks. She looked up at the group. "What's this one?"

"It's called a Ray's Mistake," said Danny. "I'm having one, too." He looked at her as he suggestively tongued the straw.

Hannah laughed and shook her head—Danny really was a shameless flirt. *Too bad I'm not turned on by cunnilingus,* she thought. Still, she couldn't help but think that she wished she was sitting next to Danny, instead of Elena. *Then again,* she thought as her head swam, *maybe it's a good thing that I'm not.*

She didn't even realize that an hour had passed until someone asked what their next stop should be. She panicked a bit—what if Connor was close by and missed them? She didn't want to say anything, for fear of seeming too desperate.

She didn't have to. Danny was watching her. When there was a break in the panoply of suggestions, he mentioned in passing, "Doesn't look like Connor's gonna make it, after all. He texted me about 20 minutes ago." He looked at her apologetically. Hannah couldn't help but be grateful that he'd waited to say something, so that she wouldn't think too much about it while she indulged in her second behemoth drink.

Dominic and his sister had driven to the Ti, and they all decided to pile into the small sedan and head over to Koreatown for some karaoke fun. The two men sat in front, and the ladies crowded into the back. It didn't seem long for Hannah until they arrived at a non-descript mini-mall on Vermont. Her head felt light as she climbed out of the car and followed the crowd into the dark karaoke parlor, and time seemed to jump as they all settled into the private room that contained a television on one wall and a U-shaped sofa on the others. Hannah looked over at Danny, who was flirting with Dominic's sister. She shook her head.

It wasn't long before staff in black button-up shirts brought plates of fried food and pitchers of milky, white fluid.

"What is that?" she asked.

Danny came to sit next to her. "It's soju." He grabbed two glasses and poured them full, handing her one. "You'll like it."

She took the glass from him and sipped. It was sweet as lemonade, and didn't taste strong at all. She figured it was safe to enjoy a glass. "That's really good!"

He laughed and tapped her glass with his own. "I told you."

Danny continued to sit next to Hannah as the other girls in the group selected songs from the many catalogs. The room became a din of loud, warped music, laughter, and off-key singing. Hannah laughed along with the others, and sang just as badly as the rest. Danny sat next to her, whispering in her ear. She kept sipping soju. Her glass stayed full, and so did his. Lady Gaga came on, and Hannah grabbed the mic and wailed out the worst rendition of "Bad Romance" ever. Danny cheered her on. At some point, they started holding hands. Hannah's hand was on Danny's thigh. He kissed the back of her neck. And the pitcher of soju was empty.

It wasn't long before they were piling back into the car, but this time Hannah sat in Danny's lap in the back seat. She could hear him talking to the others, but couldn't really make out what he was saying. But she was delighted at the smell of his neck as she nuzzled it, and could tell that he liked having her there as he squeezed her close to him.

They ended up at a dive bar with a long counter and large dance floor. Someone handed Hannah a glass of water, and she sipped it slowly with one hand as her other hand reached around Danny—she hadn't let go of him since the karaoke place. She just knew she had to be near him—nothing else mattered at the moment.

"I listened to Exquisite Corpse," she shouted into his ear. "It's really good, Danny. You should keep writing."

"No time," he shouted back into her ear. "It's too draining, anyway. But I'm glad you like it." As he finished saying it, he allowed his lips to brush the outer edge of her ear.

She let her eyes pierce into his. "There's more to you than meets the eye. And I'm glad for it." She placed the water onto a counter as Danny moved with her to the edges of the dance floor. They held each other in a long embrace, swaying to music that had no particular melody to her at the moment, although it might have been familiar. As they swayed, she realized how much shorter she was than he. She wanted to *feel* him, but her hips didn't reach. An impulse told her to climb onto him. So she did, her legs locking around his hips. He grasped onto her, surprise and delight registering on his face. She brushed her lips tantalizingly over his. *Just a taste,* she thought, *but…my, do you taste good.*

*

Danny stumbled into his apartment. He was in awe of what he'd been a witness to tonight: he had no idea that Hannah Mercury could be that hot. But, then again, she was hot and had *been* hot. It was like he'd had blinders on—and, tonight, Hannah slid them off. He wished he could slide more off—he'd got just enough of a feel for her over her skintight jeans that he longed to feel more. He felt himself throbbing hard in his pants. And then he felt a vibration.

It was his phone. A message from Hannah said, simply: *Home.* <3

Sure, he was still raw from Akie's continued rejection. But lucky for him, Hannah was here to distract him from that. And what a lovely distraction she would be.

Track 4

August had been a busy month socially, which meant that it afforded no opportunity for spontaneity or further exploration of what Danny and Hannah had experienced together. What seemed so obvious to them seemed to have been missed by every single person present that night. When Hannah had asked Tammy if she'd gone overboard with Danny, Tammy simply said, "Oh, it was a little weird that you two were so huggy, but trust me, I've seen worse." Hannah really thought she had done more than just hug—hadn't she pretty much mounted him standing? Hadn't he kissed the back of her neck?

What made it even more confusing, however, was that Danny didn't necessarily chat that much about it, either. When they got back to work the Monday after the epic happy hour, Danny had been his same, friendly, flirty self. Maybe a little more flirtatious than he had been prior to their encounter, but there were no apologies or acknowledgements of what the two had shared. Hannah was beginning to wonder if it had all been in her mind.

Anyway, two birthdays had been celebrated in the following few weeks: Tammy's and Elena's. So they enjoyed group lunches with no moment for private conversation. And it almost felt to Hannah like she wasn't supposed to go to lunch with Danny unless a group outing was planned. After all, it was a friend *group*, right? Not a pair. Was it her own self-consciousness that she didn't want to act too clingy? Or perhaps her experience with Connor?

Connor. He had pretty much stopped even communicating with her about work, now that he'd been assigned two new finance projects to which Hannah was not assigned. She felt an unbearable ache in her heart whenever she saw him, and she wished fervently that she didn't have to feel it anymore. She had wished time and again that love could just go away—knowing herself enough to know that love was like energy and could not turn to nothing.

But energy can be transferred, she thought. And a simple thought then crept into her mind. *I wish I could be in love with somebody that actually likes to be around me. Someone like Danny.*

It was then and there that she wondered if a person could consciously transfer feelings of love from someone unworthy to someone more worthy. Could love work like that?

It was toward the end of the month that Hannah found herself in a relatively empty office. Tammy was out sick. Eduardo was out-of-town at some important symposium. Elena was swamped with invoices. Dominic was on vacation. So of course she wandered over to Danny's cubicle, in search of information about the fire station as an excuse to do so.

"Hey, Danny." She stood at the opening of his cubicle.

Danny turned around. "Hey." He looked at his guest chair, which was piled with papers, and hastily moved them all to an unoccupied spot at his desk. "Here—sit down."

Hannah sat gladly. "Do we have a date to meet with the neighborhood council yet?"

"Actually—yes. Save the date for September 13th. We'll go out and make a day of it." He winked at her, stretching his legs out so that his foot touched hers. Hannah's body tingled at even the suggestion of a touch from him.

"That'll be fun. We'll have to research restaurants in the Valley. I mean, we have to eat, right?" Hannah felt her cheeks getting warm for no reason.

"Just remember, we're probably looking at a late afternoon meeting with the neighborhood council."

Hannah slid her foot to sidle up against his. "Then I guess we'll just have to plan to get up there by lunchtime—you know, to strategize?"

Danny smiled. "And then, we'll probably wanna debrief. So we should hang out there for dinner. Just so we don't forget any important points." He flexed out his legs, letting his knee touch hers.

"I think that's a smart idea." Hannah gazed at him with what certainly must be bedroom eyes. She could feel herself getting wet from his touch, and the thought of lunch and dinner with him in a single day excited her even more. Her legs were probably more open than they should be in the knee-length skirt she had on.

Suddenly, Danny glanced over Hannah's shoulder at his cubicle opening, and she heard a familiar voice. "Oh, uh—I can come back." She looked over her shoulder and saw Connor. She immediately drew her legs back to her own body and sat up straight in her chair.

Danny kept his relaxed position. "No, no—it's cool."

Hannah started to get up. "I can go."

Danny shook his head at her, and Connor said, "Real quick question—do we have any additional press releases coming up for the police station? 'Cause if we do there was some funding information I need to correct."

Hannah settled tensely back in the guest chair, feeling like she had no way out. Danny glanced at her and smiled while he answered Connor's question. "Yeah, as a matter of fact we do. Go ahead and e-mail me the changes so I can drop them in there."

Connor nodded somberly. "Will do. Thanks." And he walked away.

Hannah didn't know what to feel. Should she feel bad that Connor saw her flirting with Danny? Glad? Her body was still throbbing for Danny—a feeling that Connor had once given her, but which now was impossible around him because of the heartache. And whose fault was that? Hers for telling her husband? Connor's for not trying harder?

She shook her head. "Did you see that? He didn't even acknowledge my existence."

Danny waved his hand as if to pass it off. "They're all just tense over this police station thing. It's gonna be the new headache. Which is good for me—keep 'em rolling in, keep me employed. I'm not a civil servant like you—I'm exempt, at will. So the more work the better."

Hannah looked down at her lap. "I'm glad for your sake. But, Danny—we were really close less than a year ago. He can't even say hi?"

"He *can* be a little strange." He reached out his foot and touched her toe. "Try not to think about it. Come on, you were so relaxed before!"

Hannah managed a little smile. "It's hard not to think about it."

"You know, I think you just need to get out again. Maybe we should do another happy hour, just a few of us."

"Yeah, probably not a good idea this soon after the last. My husband wasn't exactly thrilled about how late I got back."

Danny frowned. "You're an adult. You should be able to go out with some friends without having to feel like you're doing something wrong. What does he need, a play-by-play?"

Hannah tilted her head. "He's still raw from what happened with Connor…I can't really blame him. I mean, here I am, saddling him with the kids while I go out and get drunk."

"You have a right to a night out."

Hannah raised her eyebrows. "Maybe so, but I also have an obligation to him, even if we are separated. And to my kids. Anyway, I just want to give him a little space from the last one before I ask him if I can do it again…But, hey—why wait for after work? There's nobody here today, and I have a free lunch.

Danny's eyes lit up. "You ever been to Wurstküche?"

Wurstküche was a casual lunch place in the Arts District. It served sausages and beer. Hannah had always theorized that men brought women there so they could see them eat the sausages. That Danny suggested it seemed like it could be laced with innuendo—or he could just want a beer.

They took Danny's SUV and were lucky to find street parking. Hannah chose a vegetarian sausage and a dark Koestrizer. Danny got rattlesnake and a less intimidating hef. They found a seat in the stripped-down dining area. Hannah looked across at her friend. "Thanks for suggesting this. I really needed to get out of there."

"It was long overdue for us to do lunch again, just the two of us," said Danny. "It's nice." The server dropped their food order at the table.

"Plus, you get to watch me stuff a sausage in my mouth," teased Hannah, eyebrow raised.

Danny laughed. "Added plus. After all, you really think I'm ever gonna get to watch you do more?"

Hannah chugged her Koestrizer. "Don't bet on it." They both eyed each other, knowing that at the moment that bet might have 50/50 odds. Hannah blushed. "So, do you have a name for the band yet?"

"Yeah, but it sucks."

"How bad can it be?" Hannah leaned in for the answer.

Danny looked away, chuckling. "Montage."

Hannah wrinkled her nose. "Oh—yeah. That's pretty bad."

"Terrible." Danny was shaking his head.

"Sounds like the name of one of those new housing developments."

"Yep."

"Solar panels, optional barbecue pit."

"Easy freeway access." Danny swigged his beer.

"Did you tell the guys what you thought about it?"

"I did."

"And?"

"Our name is still Montage."

Hannah gritted her teeth. "Yikes. Well—then the music better be that good. Are you writing anything new for the band?"

"Nope." He took a gigantic bite of his rattlesnake.

"Why not?"

He washed his bite down with some beer and then looked at Hannah. "I guess I just haven't been inspired yet."

"What about that girl?"

"Which one?"

"You know which one. What's her name?"

He polished off his drink. "Akie. And I guess she hasn't really inspired me to write anything."

Hannah considered this. The love of your life not inspiring you? But she thought it might sound a little self-serving to question it. Add to that, she was way behind Danny on eating her food. The beer had really filled her up. She decided to change the subject. "Well, I don't know if I can finish this. Do you want any?"

"Sure." He took a big bite.

Hannah leaned back on the bench seat. "Danny, I am so buzzed. I can't go back to work like this."

"Okay, let's go get some coffee after this, okay?"

Hannah wrinkled her nose. "I don't like coffee."

"We can go to Urth and you can get some tea."

"Sounds good," Hannah said as she shot up out of her seat.

Danny laughed. "Ready to go?"

Hannah nodded and walked toward the back exit. Danny followed her, opening the door as they left. Once outside, he snuck his arm around her waist. Hannah put her arm around his and leaned into him. "This is so much fun."

Danny squeezed her tight. "See, we can do one-on-one. This is a nice little lunch date."

His comment made Hannah sad for a second. She remembered Connor saying almost exactly that the first night they had gone out together. He'd said that he was having more fun than some dates he had been on. But the fun hadn't lasted. Her heart felt heavy for a few moments, until Danny stopped her.

"Hey, this is my car, remember?"

Hannah was happily pulled back to the present moment. "You mean your crossover?"

He opened the passenger door for her. "Yeah, my crossover."

She remained standing next to him, arms still entwined around each other. "Are we driving to Urth?"

"A bit far to walk, don't you think?"

She gave him a last squeeze and then settled into the car. "That's a very Angelino thing to say. But you're the one that has to drive, so I'm in your hands."

He walked around to the driver's seat and settled in. "You're in good hands, trust me."

"I trust you." The drive to Urth took less than five minutes, and once again they scored a good parking spot. They went inside and ordered a regular latte for him, a tea latte for her. Sitting on the patio, they bounced around other band names, deciding that any one of them would be better than Montage.

After about a half hour, Danny looked at his watch. "You ready to head back?"

Hannah had her hand on her chin, and was feeling much more balanced. "No. But I suppose we should." They got up and walked toward the car. At one point their hands became entwined, and broke only to get back into the car. The drive back to the office was short, uneventful, and—for Hannah, at least—filled with contentment. Once they'd parked the SUV in the office lot and were walking towards the door to their building (hands off), Hannah once again allowed herself to speak. "This was fun. Let's not wait too long until we do it again."

"How about next week?"

Hannah was pleasantly surprised that he was as eager to spend time together as she was. "Next week sounds perfect!"

"And what will be on the menu next week?"

Hannah hesitated. "Well—you might think it's a bit far…"

"Far? Where is it?"

"It's this breakfast place in Hollywood. It's been on my Yelp list for ages, but I've never had occasion to go."

Danny winked. "Well, you have occasion now. When you said far, I thought you meant like the beach or something."

She laughed. "Well, I do know a few good breakfast places on the Westside—but let's stick to Hollywood for now."

No one seemed to notice that the two had been gone for two hours—or if they did, no one said anything. And despite the length of their absence for lunch, Hannah felt so much more focused and productive the rest of that afternoon. It was like she was calming that twitch within her, the one that needed escape from the confinement of these beige partitions and to live life a little. And when it got the escape it needed, it quieted and allowed her to do what she had to in order to maintain the other 99% of her existence.

*

A week passed—work, eating, mothering, weekend with family, life…and yet Hannah could not help but look forward primarily to the next outing she and Danny had scheduled together.

She realized how desperate this feeling had become when it came time to select Halloween costumes for herself and the children. Halloween had always been a huge deal for Hannah: she sewed costumes for the kids, enlisted her husband to construct non-fabric elements to the costumes, and dutifully created a mock-graveyard in the front of their small suburban house. She even took half a day off from work, so that she could still show off her costume among the cubicles, but get home in time for some serious trick-or-treating. She started planning for it weeks in advance, and this year was no exception. Last year had been the first year that her husband and she hadn't done a romantic couple's costume, like Henry VIII and Anne Boleyn or Salome and John the Baptist: those days were done the minute he had found out about her and Connor, and in retrospect she had always selected such ill-fated lovers, anyway. But she had resolved that she'd do team costumes with the children. They'd done a Harry Potter theme, with her husband as Dumbledore, the kids as Harry and Hermione, and herself sporting a Bellatrix Lestrange getup. She had gotten the makeup especially grue-some and demented.

She turned to her son Monday night while cooking dinner. "So what's our theme for Halloween this year?" He was always the primary source for ideas in their family.

He scrunched his little face in deep thought. Then his eyes lit up and he blurted, "Zombies!"

Hannah laughed but then paused for a second. She knew she want-ed to dress in something sort of sexy and mildly risqué for Halloween this year, so that Danny could see her and maybe fantasize a little about what was underneath. Rotting zombie skin and torn, tattered clothing would in no way yield any such result. "Hmmm...I think your sister would be a little frightened of zombie makeup. Maybe we go with something not quite so scary, like...X-Men?"

Her son frowned for a second, but then nodded in agreement. "Okay, but I get to be Wolverine."

She tried to tell herself that the choice was in the interest of not scaring her daughter—and she almost believed it. But, deep down, she knew that Danny was starting to affect even something as simple as what she chose for her kids to be for Halloween.

It felt distinctly as if she was in the process of creating two lives for herself: the one that she lived most of the time, and the one that she lived those collective 2 to 3 precious hours every week that she could talk to, eat with, or just be near Danny. And she was trying desperately to make sure those 2 to 3 hours counted. She convinced herself that what she was doing was a good thing, because without it she would surely be despairing over the loss of the temporary and unsustainable relationship she'd shared with Connor. She was willing herself to create something that maybe felt a little bit like love so that she didn't have to come to terms with the true and heartbreaking love that she'd lost. And she ignored the remote voice that spoke at the back of her mind, the one that told her that what she had with Danny could also not possibly last—because if it couldn't last, she didn't want to spend her present days dreading its end.

*

The breakfast place was on Sunset, but Danny parked on a residential street to avoid metered parking. As he shifted the car into "Park", he looked over to take in his charming companion. She had worn skintight pleather-like jeans and a scoop-neck, tight shirt that showed a nice amount of cleavage. It peaked out under the light jacket she had zipped up before they left. She looked kinda rock 'n' roll—it was a different look for her, and she looked really hot. He wondered if he'd had anything to do with that—he hoped he did.

He'd been looking forward to this all week, even cleaning the car so that it would look good for her. It seemed important to put his best foot forward for her, give her a little of the royal treatment. After all, this was not just some chick that he'd met at a bar or in a club. This was Hannah—his friend. She was and deserved to be treated like a lady. And because of this, he'd decided after the night of that epic happy hour that it was best to slow things down a bit. He knew Hannah was still raw from that thing that happened with Connor, and although he didn't know the details, he knew from his own experience with Akie how rushing things could be a fast-track to complete break-down. And he really wanted to ride this one as long as he could.

He was glad he'd peeked at the weather forecast before he left for work and stuck an umbrella in the back. Although the sun had been shining that morning, as they drove down the 101 clouds closed the sky in a curtain of steely grey. It was unseasonable weather for the beginning of September, but then again these days nothing was predictable where the weather was concerned. He'd just finished sweeping his eyes over Hannah when drops of water started to hit the windshield.

She glanced out the window. "Uh-oh—I'm glad I have a waterproof jacket on!"

He felt proud to be able to say, "No worries—I have an umbrella in the back. Lemme get it for you." He zipped up the light windbreaker that he always wore and stepped out as the rain pelted harder. He wanted to be sure to do this just right, so when he got the umbrella out he didn't open it for himself. He waited until he got to her door, and unlatched it before giving a little valet care to his favorite little lunch date.

She looked grateful as she stepped out of the car. "Oh, Danny—you're getting soaked. Let's share."

Just like a pimp, he thought smugly to himself. He made sure to hold the umbrella completely over her, and only allowed his hand to brush her shoulder lightly before hastily removing it.

She smiled at him under the umbrella. "You can keep it there. I don't mind." He smiled back—who was the pimp now? He wasn't so sure, but if he had to put money on it, he'd probably say it was Hannah.

They walked into a very crowded restaurant. Hannah gave her name to the host and they were directed to wait in the back hall. There were lots of hipsters and some seats back there, and the two friends settled comfortably, leaning into each other as seemed to be their habit every time they had the opportunity.

"I had a weird run-in with that guy from systems," said Hannah.

Danny laughed. "Uh-oh. What happened?"

"He gave me a CD of music. It was nice, but I was kind of in a rush and had to sort of subtly get him to leave me alone so that I could finish my work. I don't want to seem mean, but I just didn't have time to chat. I knew we were going out and I really wanted to get as much done as I could, so that I didn't feel guilty if we run long. He always seems to catch me at the worst times."

Danny shrugged. "You don't gotta apologize for anything. Hot chicks got their own problems, and there's no way that dude's gonna understand, anyway. You can't let guys like that get the wrong impression, or you will be getting a lot more CD's."

Hannah raised her eyebrows. "Really, you think I'm a hot chick?"

Danny had heard this sort of baiting before. "Come on, you know you're hot."

Hannah gave him that direct and honest gaze that told him she was telling the truth. "No, I don't."

He was surprised. "How can you not know you're hot?"

"I don't know—I just never got that from anyone before. You're the first person I've known that ever told me I was hot."

"Wow. That's surprising." What the hell was wrong with dudes? How could someone like Hannah be made to feel like she was ordinary?

"Anyway, I guess you're right about not apologizing, because I really just get this super creepy vibe when he gives me something." She paused, as if considering something. "Please let me know if I'm ever that creepy." Hannah nudged him with her shoulder.

"If you were that creepy, I wouldn't be here." He smiled at her, glad for this gift the universe had given him in knowing her.

The host called her name, and the two sat down with a legion of hipsters and tourists to indulge in trendy brunch food. They enjoyed a shared meal of red velvet pancakes and eggs benedict. They ate until they were stuffed. When they were done, he looked over the counter at her. "So was it as good as you thought?"

She patted her belly. "Better—so worth the wait!" He imagined she would be, too.

Danny knew he wasn't ready to go back to work. So as they left the restaurant, he asked an open-ended question. "Anywhere else you wanna go?"

A mischievous grin took over her face. "I *have* been wanting to go to Amoeba…"

"Amoeba it is!" said Danny, before she could think that she was asking too much. They spent half an hour walking together among the CD and record shelves of the world-famous (and somewhat dinosaur-like) megastore, making comments about bands and music and other fun stuff. A lunch with Hannah was like a sweet little break from life.

*

It turned out that the neighborhood council meeting was at 5:00 p.m., and both their workloads too busy to have lunch before. The two ended up getting to the meeting five minutes before it started; and although they both felt after that they had made some serious headway in turning the tide as far as public opinion was concerned, there was still

enough resistance to make Hannah worry about what would happen
when the matter was, once again, placed before City Council. It didn't
seem appropriate or wise to have dinner in the area, since so many
people they had met would also be around. Both Hannah and Danny
were obliged to operate completely professionally and above-board.
Hannah was disappointed, but Danny promised to make sure to set
aside time for an extra-long lunch the next week.

And he came through on his promise. When the next Wednesday
arrived, Danny chatted Hannah first thing.

"Danny: Ready for that lunch?"

"Hannah: Yep-so excited!"

"Danny: Any ideas?"

"Hannah: There's a pub in Hollywood, looks pretty cool."

"Danny: Sounds good! 11:30?"

"Hannah: Perfect. TTYL."

The Pikey was situated on Sunset Boulevard, in an old building that
had been operating, off and on, as a pub for over 75 years. Hannah kept
up a constant stream of casual chatter along the way from the office,
commenting on billboards and storefronts, peppered with plenty of
innuendo. She had worn a black button-up blouse and a crimson red
wiggle skirt with a side slit that was just barely work-appropriate. She
hoped that it would make Danny want to touch her. They parked on a
quiet, tree-lined residential drive, then walked up to the establishment's
red door. Once seated, Hannah ordered an Absinthe drink—she'd
never had one before, and it sounded exotic and romantic to her. A few
sips relaxed her mind, and freed her tongue to ask the sorts of questions
she always felt she couldn't ask.

"So what do you want from life, Danny—really *want?*"

Danny gave a smirk that showed he hadn't consumed enough of his
bourbon yet. "What do you want?"

Hannah stretched in the dark wooden booth. "I don't know. For a long time I thought I knew what I wanted, back when I was in school and the world seemed so open. Did you know that I wanted to be in marketing, like you?"

Danny raised his eyebrows. "No, I didn't know that."

"Yeah, well—it didn't work out. Now that I just sort of fell into the work that I do, I guess I'm sort of committed to stick with it. Grow in the division—maybe manage someday. I don't know if the 'what' I do really matters that much anymore, not now that life has gotten so…well, so complicated."

"You feel your life is complicated?" Danny was steadily swigging throughout Hannah's comments.

"More than it was before I got involved with—well, you know." Hannah blushed, then looked down. "Before that—well, I guess I just saw my future as it related to being a wife and mother. I didn't think much about what *I* really wanted. It never seemed to matter, as long as my husband and kids were okay. I took a job that I knew would pay enough so that I could maintain a comfortable lifestyle for them. I bought a house in a part of L.A. County that wasn't ever my ideal, because I knew the schools were good, a house that didn't have everything I wanted because I felt pressured to hurry up and get into the housing market. I always lived by the ocean growing up, and I always hated that we ended up in such a dry, arid place. It took years for my skin to adapt…Then that whole Connor thing happened, and all of a sudden, I realized that I wasn't thinking *enough* about what I wanted all along. That's probably *why* it happened. I've spent so much of my young adulthood just worrying about how to be the perfect wife and mother that I lost sight of who I was, essentially. So I started doing things that were not at all like me. I guess if you lose track of who you are enough, or don't cultivate it enough, boredom just sort of sets in and takes over—and you open yourself up to anything happening, instead of the things you plan or want."

Danny nodded his head. If he wasn't truly intrigued by what she was saying, at least he played well enough at it. "So what does that leave you with?"

She shrugged. "Well, it leaves me with a house that I don't quite love in an area that I'm not crazy about, that I can't sell because I'm still underwater on the loan. It leaves me with a job that was never what I really wanted." She sighed. "So I have new goals—adaptive goals, I guess. Grow in the job that I have, and be the best that I can. Move someday to an area nearer the basin, so that I can be closer to the things I love to do. Maybe somewhere close to the beach. If I can't do what I want professionally, at least I can get closer to an area where I can do what I want socially. My husband and I are still living together. I guess that makes things easier for the kids right now, but it's not the ideal situation, now that we're separated. Not if we're not going to make it..." She looked piercingly at Danny. It always frustrated her how a question she posed always seemed to end with her opening her heart and Danny's mouth staying shut. "So, come on—what do you want, Danny?"

He chuckled. "Stay employed."

"And then what?"

"Worry about music instead of money. Work to make the band better, crappy name and all. Record. Perform."

Hannah raised one eyebrow. "Write?"

Danny waved down the waiter to get another bourbon. "No. Not right now."

"But you're so good at it! You know, I really liked your music, especially that one slower song that you wrote about the unexpected moment that you had with someone. It really affected me...Who did you write it about?"

Danny shrugged. "I don't really like to tell people who I write my songs about. It's better if the song is left open for the listener to interpret."

Hannah could feel herself getting a little frustrated. She'd confided so much to him—she thought he might return the favor. "I think the listener could still interpret it, even if they knew the backstory. A good song is still relatable."

"Yeah, maybe—but once you know what it's about I think it doesn't quite have the same—open-endedness? Anyway, I always preferred not to know. There were so many songs that I heard, growing up, that I don't think would have had the same effect if I had known exactly what they were about."

Hannah sipped her Absinthe drink again. "Like what?"

"Oh, like *Sweet Child of Mine*, for instance. I know it's a man singing about a woman, but when I was younger I thought about it more like it was a mother and a son. Growing up, it was just me and my mom. My dad was sort of—well, let's just say he was out of the picture. Life wasn't easy—we were poor, sometimes not sure what to eat. But we had each other. And that song made me think of how life always felt like it was me and my mom against the world—and that maybe someone else had gone through the same thing."

Hannah was surprised. "You never told me about that."

"I don't like to talk about it much. It was hard to be the only kid that couldn't play because he had to go home to help mom pay the bills. Or because I had to get home before it got dark, because we didn't pay them soon enough and they turned our power off again and I needed to be able to finish my homework in the natural light." He polished off the second bourbon.

"So music has always been there for you."

"Sometimes more than people. People have always let me down. Music has always brought me up." He looked piercingly at Hannah.

"I hope I never let you down, Danny."

He smiled. "I think you're more like a song to me. You always bring me up."

Hannah blushed, and felt her heart swell. She wanted to bring him up, make him happy. She wanted to be someone that he could think about and smile. She felt honored that she could be that to him.

The Absinthe had done its job. Hannah felt as light as air. When they were finished eating, they explored the old pub a bit. There was a big room in back that looked like it could be used for special events. There was a bar on the other side that would be perfect for a future happy hour. When they finally wandered out, Danny placed his arm around her waist, and she felt happy and adored and whole. As they walked along the little residential side street, she looked up and appreciated the canopy of trees that sheltered the street.

Danny opened the door for her, and then got into the driver's side. But instead of starting the car, he reclined his seat. "Perfect day…" he mused.

Hannah felt moved to snuggle into his arms. "I'm glad I could give you a perfect day."

"We made it together." He kissed the top of her head. "You know I don't want anything from you, right?"

Hannah kissed his shoulder. "I know."

"We're just having some fun. I'm not trying to get in on what you have with your husband or Connor—and you're not trying to get in on what I have with Akie."

She smiled. "I hardly have time for anything more than fun. I know you want to be with Akie. And as for me and Connor—well, I think that ship has sailed. I think I'm going to focus my energy on working things out with my husband." She tilted her head up to brush her lips against his neck. "But today is lovely."

He put his hand on her exposed thigh and squeezed. "I wish we could run away for the rest of the day...Just you and me, chilling on the beach. Looking at your ocean."

Hannah closed her eyes and imagined them sitting there together in the sand. Santa Monica, or maybe Venice. "I can think of nothing more wonderful." She looked up from her daydream, and saw the trees above the car, and his well-manicured beard right above her face: her daydream right before her eyes. She was tempted to kiss that pouty lip that protruded above his beard—she settled for tracing it with her finger. So soft. He smiled. Perfect day, indeed.

*

Things were definitely looking up with regards to the fire station. Council had approved the project to move forward with the bid process, with very little objection from the community, and it appeared as though the extension they had requested from the Feds would buy them additional time to go through that process. Danny was informed that he was to stay on for at least another six months, since the funding was now secure and he would still be needed to retain public approval as the project moved into the construction phase. And his continued work with the new police station seemed to be presenting him with additional PR challenges.

Even so, in the weeks following, Hannah and Danny escaped to lunch together several more times; sometimes on a Thursday, but most of the time on Wednesdays. Thursdays were preserved for keeping their public face with the rest of the group. No one suspected a thing. Definitely not a testament to their discretion, Hannah thought. They cavorted through the Roosevelt Hotel, hand in hand. They gazed at each other on the patio of Alcove. Hollywood. Silverlake. The Arts

District. They snuck around right in plain sight. It was a thrill to be fun and young and slightly irresponsible.

They always ended up in each other's arms—a squeeze of the thigh, a brush of lips on the cheek. They even shared a crazy subway ride as she tried to arouse him by brushing up against his jeans as they stood, face to face, in the rocking car (a challenge because of his height, but she smiled thinking of the way he had to discreetly adjust himself, nonetheless). It hadn't gone too far beyond these relatively innocuous touches—but then again it wasn't necessarily helping her commit 100% to her husband, either. She thought every week that this would surely be the last; but then they both kept coming back for more. And every time they did, she knew it was making it that much harder to stop.

Halloween morning brought anticipation and a little nervousness for Hannah. Her kids had the day off from school, and convinced her to let them visit the office for half a day. It wasn't ever a problem in her department to bring her kids every once in a while, and management was very family-oriented. But when she had absentmindedly agreed to taking the children along, she had somewhat forgotten that this meant Danny would now be meeting her kids, and a major component of Hannah's careful compartmentalization of her life would be dissolved. She worried that maybe Danny seeing her as a "mom" would shatter his illusion of her as an object of desire. With mixed feelings, she eased into the skintight, red zipper catsuit that she had purchased.

They must have been an amusing sight, her son striding confidently in front in his yellow Wolverine costume, Hannah walking somewhat apologetically in a red Phoenix getup, and her daughter staying cautiously close in a green Rogue outfit.

Tammy was the first to see them. "What! You guys look amazing!"

"I'm Wolverine!" shouted Hannah's son.

Tammy played along. "Good, because I need someone to save me from the bad guys. They're everywhere around here."

"I'll tear through 'em with my adamantium claws!"

"If only, sweetie, if only...Well, Miss Phoenix, look at you! Should I infer anything from you choosing the bad side of Jean Grey?" Tammy raised her eyebrows suggestively.

Hannah laughed. "Just wanted to distinguish myself from Rogue here." Her daughter moved closer. "She's still worried that her alias will be blown."

Tammy smiled. "Who isn't?"

Hannah prodded the kids towards Danny's cubicle. "Come on, guys, there's someone I want you to meet."

She was glad to see that Danny was working diligently when she knocked on his partition. He turned around, and a huge smile spread across his face when he saw the three of them. "It's the X-Men!"

She giggled. "Well, three of us, anyway. Wolverine and Rogue, I want you to meet Danny."

Her son looked up at Danny confidently. "If you're a bad guy, I'll claw you."

Danny burst into laughter. "I'll remember that." He kneeled in front of Hannah's daughter, holding out his hand. "I'm so pleased to meet you, Rogue."

She giggled. "That's not my *real* name."

"Well, how about you tell me your real name only once you're confident that I'm a good guy?" She nodded her head, and shook his hand. Danny discreetly eyed Hannah up-and-down. "Same goes for you, Phoenix."

"Well, then I guess you'll never know my real name," she mused. "My mutant instincts are telling me to look out for you." The kids jumped out of Danny's cubicle and assumed full make-believe mode. "I guess I better go after them and make sure they don't tear the place apart."

Danny winked. "All for the better. Otherwise I might start to be a bad guy just so we can spar."

Hannah put her hands on her hips. "Well, remember—Phoenix is a little bad, too."

Danny licked his upper lip. "Just the way I like my superheroes."

Laughing as she walked away, Hannah couldn't help but feel a bit triumphant. Even wrangling two tiny superheroes, she still felt completely desirable to Danny. Her being a mother didn't appear to be a deterrent at all. She hoped he enjoyed watching her walk away, knowing that she'd be back.

*

Hannah breathed in deep, imagining Danny's smell late one afternoon. She could recall it in an instant, so familiar was he to her now. She looked at the clock on her computer. 5:30—she was supposed to stay until 7:00. But nobody was left except a few random staff that weren't tracking her comings and goings. And Danny. She went over to his workspace. He was looking at the Ticketmaster website. "Done for the day?"

He turned and smiled. "Just about, but I got practice tonight so I'm pretty much just sitting around 'til 7:30."

She sighed. "I'm supposed to stay until 7:00, but I'm so done. I think I'll just come in super-early tomorrow. You want some company?" She settled into his guest chair.

Danny smiled. "You know, we could go have a quick drink."

She beamed. "I was thinking the exact same thing. Where?"

"Maybe we should do something close to the train station. What time is your train?"

"I drove in. So we can go somewhere that's close to your practice space. That way, we have more time to drink." She winked the way he always did at her.

He laughed. "Okay—I'll pick something close enough for me, close to the freeway for you. Let me wrap things up here and I'll send you a link to the address. We'll meet there."

"Okay." Hannah wandered back to her desk to pack things up. Within minutes he chatted her the link to a dive bar in Echo Park. She felt her heart pounding. Something told her she was going to keep this one on the serious DL.

The Gold Room was on Sunset Boulevard. He was waiting for her outside the place. "It looks pretty cool in there. I peeked inside." He opened the door. She smiled at him as she entered. He was right—it was about as dive as it gets. And it was fairly empty, too.

He ordered a $4 beer and shot of tequila, and she got a whiskey sour. She indicated the booths between the window and the bar, and he took a seat. She sat right next to him, draping her patent vinyl boots over his lap. There was no time to dance around it tonight. They were both there for the exact same reason, and she wanted to get as drunk as she could as quickly as she could so she could act the way she wanted to act when she was sober, but for which she could only have an excuse if she was drunk. The setting sun was streaming through the window at that moment, and he gazed appreciatively.

"You're amazing."

She placed her free hand on his thigh. "Thank you." They both drank some more, talking about things that she would never remember and that didn't matter tonight. She got up to use the bathroom. He reached his hand between her legs, over her voluminous skirt, and felt where she was already throbbing. She turned to glance at him. "I'll be right back."

When she returned, she felt free to kiss his neck, biting a little along the way. He gave a sharp intake of breath, then pulled at her hair so he could see her face. He looked absolutely entranced. She whispered into his ear. "You like it rough? So do I." She wished she could mount him right there.

He whispered in her ear. "We have to be careful. We don't wanna get kicked out." And with that, he probed his tongue into her ear. It seemed to her a way for him to express that, even though he was holding her back, he still wanted to have something inside of her. Hannah thought to herself that it was sort of adolescent and gross, but at the same time arousing. She throbbed with wanting him.

But, as was always the case with them, she was minding the time. And it looked like it was getting close to the time when they must go their separate ways. "When do you need to go?" she asked him.

He looked at his watch. "Probably about now. You just about done?"

"I'm good," she said, even though deep down she wished he didn't have to go to practice, and she didn't have to go home.

"I'll walk you to your car."

They said very little as they walked the block to her minivan. But when they got to the car and embraced, she was moved to speak. "I want to kiss you."

He touched his nose to hers and said, "Peck." So she gave him an innocent peck on the lips. It was as if that little gesture was meant to hold back the flood of passion that flowed through her body. She thought to herself that it worked for now. But she wasn't sure how long it would be before the dam ruptured.

Track 5

Hannah couldn't stop thinking about sex, and Danny wasn't helping. Not that he could. For all the excitement the two had shared before Thanksgiving, the holiday season had been dead as far as their relationship—if you could even call it that—was concerned. Hannah didn't think that she could call it that. But Danny couldn't help it. He'd gone on a backpacking expedition in Amsterdam the week of Thanksgiving, and had been inundated with police station business ever since his return. Hannah had tried to get him out of the office, but he was so focused on his work that he didn't seem to want to make time for her. She tried not to be hurt—after all, their agreement was to have fun together, not to have some sort of dating relationship. And he didn't have time for fun. But still she missed him.

She'd actually been trying to work things out with her estranged husband. Her unconsummated relationship with Danny had left her so in need of sex that the proximity had opened itself up to opportunity. It had started after they had put the kids to bed one evening. Hannah didn't usually stay up after that, but after lying in bed for almost an hour she realized she couldn't sleep—she was too sexually frustrated from her suspended flirting with Danny. She walked into the shared living room as her husband was watching a sex documentary on television. When he noticed her, he quickly moved to change the channel, but Hannah put her hand on top of the remote.

"Leave it—it looks like it might be kind of fun to watch." She settled on the sofa next to him. A woman on the screen was talking about helping married men fulfill their sex fantasies, because their uptight wives wouldn't do it for them. The scene cut to that woman giving a blow job to a man she had tied up, whose face was tiled over to protect his identity. Hannah mused to herself whether his penis wasn't just as much of a dead giveaway to his wife, but then realized that his wife's lack of being able to be that close to the man was exactly why he was on this show. She watched as the sex-fantasy-fulfiller allowed him to "free" himself from the ties and "force" her to submit to him. The lady on the program pretended to resist as he grabbed her hair and fucked her from behind. It made Hannah think about how Danny had grabbed her hair and grabbed under her skirt.

She looked over at her husband. "Did you ever have any fantasies that I didn't fulfill?"

He smiled a little sheepishly, but quickly said, "I always enjoyed the sex."

Hannah frowned. "Okay, but that's not what I said. Did you have any fantasies?"

He shrugged. "More fellatio would have been nice."

Hannah looked at the screen. "Like that?"

"I don't need to be tied up."

Hannah imagined what it would be like to have Danny's cock in her mouth. Just the thought of it thrilled her to the point where she throbbed. It actually made her want to suck any cock. "Do you want to try now?"

Her husband looked surprised. "Really?"

"I'm kind of super horny." She laid her hand over his pajama pants, where she could tell an erection was forming.

"Are you sure you want to—with me?"

She pulled him up out of his place next to her on the sofa, so that he was standing in front of her, and pulled the pajama pants down. The sight of an erect penis made her hungry, and she dove right in and started sucking like she never had before. Giving blow jobs had just never appealed to her, but the simple thought of Danny suddenly made her need it like she never needed it before. Her husband instinctively placed his hand on her head. She closed her eyes and imagined Danny pulling her hair, and his tongue in her ear. She moaned.

Her husband was breathless. "Oh, my—you—how are you this good at that?"

Hannah could hear the moaning as another sex fantasy was being played out on the documentary. She separated her mouth from the cock in front of her. "I just was watching that and all of a sudden wanted to try it." It wasn't *completely* a lie. Kneeling like the woman in the documentary, she pulled her pajama pants and panties down and arched her back. Her husband knew exactly what to do. Entering her from behind, he copied what they'd both seen on the television, pulling her hair while he expertly stroked her.

And it was satisfying—after all, nobody knew Hannah's sex spots better than her husband. But something seemed wrong, because every moment she was close to orgasm, she felt her body resist until she imagined it was Danny that was touching her. As soon as she closed her eyes and imagined that it was him prodding her from behind, she came harder than she ever had before.

After a similar interlude in mid-December, Hannah spent the next morning more emotionally vulnerable than she could ever remember having been. It was as if the more she had orgasmed the night before, the more physical satisfaction she had received, the hungrier the next morning for emotional fulfillment, which could not truly be realized as long as Danny kept himself scarce. She decided to keep to herself: the less interaction with others, even Danny, the better.

It figured, then, that the moment she removed herself from her workspace to grab some hot water for tea, the person who came upon her in the kitchen would be Connor. She decided to try to smile at him, hoping maybe he would return this olive branch she offered. After all, they were approaching the two-year anniversary of their brief but intense time together. But instead he looked right past her, warmly greeting another (attractive) woman that worked in the office on his way out. It should not have come as any surprise to Hannah, but somehow it hit her particularly hard, and she found herself fighting back unwanted tears. She hastily returned with her tea to her cubicle, and hoped to get lost in her work. Why Danny would chose that moment to initiate an online chat was beyond her: it was like he sensed her loneliness.

"Danny: Hey H-how r u?"

"Hannah: Fine. Trying to work."

"Danny: Busy?"

"Hannah: Trying to be."

"Danny: No need to stress, right? No pressure with the holidays right around the corner."

"Hannah: Great. More reminders of not being wanted."

"Danny: ???"

"Hannah: I wouldn't expect you to get it."

"Danny: Wanna talk?"

"Hannah: Not right now. Gotta work."

"Danny: Ok. TTYL."

Hannah looked at their chat conversation a few times. She knew Danny was just trying to be friendly, but she couldn't help but be angry with him. After all, he was partially to blame for how unwanted she felt right now. After everything that they had been through, why wasn't he eager to get together again? Why did *she* seem to be the only one that cared? It was like Connor, all over again. Another Christmastime failure. She had to get away from her workspace—she could feel that the tears were going to burst out, so long had she been repressing them. She started to walk quickly toward the bathroom, head down. She did not see Danny until she ran right into him.

He laughed. "Hey, turbo, slow down there!"

She looked up at him, tears already streaming down her face. "I have to get…" she could not finish. Her tears choked her up too much.

"Whoa! Hannah, what's wrong?" He placed his hands on her shoulders. His touch made her sob uncontrollably. She missed him so much. He placed a strong arm around her back, guiding her toward the elevator lobby. "I think you need some fresh air—come on." They got into the elevator, which was mercifully empty, and he led her out onto the back plaza of their office building, and guided her onto one of the uncomfortable chairs, taking a seat in the one right next to it. "You wanna tell me what's going on?"

Hannah looked up at Danny. The concerned look in his eyes made her sob uncontrollably again. Her shoulders shook with the intensity of her sobbing. He put his hand on her knee. How could she possibly tell him what she felt? That she felt so empty since they had ceased to make their regular lunches? That all she wanted in the world was to have one more moment, and then one more moment with him? That she had uncontrollably been spiraling into an adoration for him that surpassed anything she had ever felt for Connor? She fumbled lamely for some words. "I…saw Connor today…he—he wouldn't even look at me!"

His face looked pained for her. "Oh, Hannah, I'm so sorry."

She decided to keep everything she said completely general. "After everything we shared, h-how can he just act like nothing ever happened? How can he s-see me and treat me like nothing? I'm the s-same person I was before. I haven't changed that much, have I?" She looked at him desperately.

Danny shook his head. "Oh, Hannah, it isn't you. What he's doing—Hannah, it's not normal, okay? Normal people don't act like that."

Hannah continued to sob. "I don't understand why it still matters to me. Why can't I care as little as he does?"

"Because you are normal—you can't just let the whole thing go that easily." He patted her knee. "I hate to say it, but it sounds like you got your heart broken."

Hannah looked regretfully at Danny. She wanted to tell him her heart was breaking right now, and he was the one obliviously stepping on it. But instead she just said, "Is that what this is?" She realized that it was cold outside, and she hadn't had a coat on when they left. She hugged herself against the crisp morning air.

He removed his hand from her knee. "Let's get outta here today, okay? I have a 1:30 meeting, but I'll take you somewhere early." He looked at his watch. "It's 10:30. Why don't you go and clean up, have some tea, and then we'll get going?"

She nodded, and wiped her eyes with both hands. "Thank you, Danny."

He helped her up. "Hey, what are friends for, right?"

More tears burst from her eyes. He was so good to her—it wasn't his fault that she was falling fast and hard. She knew the rules—and he was giving her his friendship right now. As much as her heart ached for him, she decided she was grateful for it, and put her arm around him. "Thank you for being such a good friend, Danny."

They had their first hands-off lunch that day, and as much as it made Hannah's whole body throb to be so close to him and yet so unable to touch him, she convinced herself that it was for the better. She never wanted what they had to become as damaged as she and Connor had become. She was glad she'd kept her true feelings to herself. If the sexual tension was challenging, she resolved to do her best to just push it aside and move forward as friends. The alternative was unimaginable.

*

Danny couldn't believe how fast time seemed to be moving, ever since Hannah had come into his life. He was anticipating the return of Akie in January, and the lovely distraction of his beautiful friend had made the past few months glide by smoothly. He really hoped he could convince Akie to stay this time around. He had so much more to offer, now that his job was fairly stable and he was closer to being a part of the music business again—his band was really picking up. Gavin had managed to book a gig at one of the biggest venues for up-and-coming bands. Maybe Akie would be back in time to see it.

He took a trip to visit his mom back home the week after his lunch with Hannah. It was nice to be reminded that he was a part of a family, not just some island of his own in Los Angeles. It felt good to be connected through that shared history. So many of his newest connections had been based in sexual attraction, and he felt like his eyes opened to the world when he was part of something bigger. He wondered why Hannah didn't feel similarly connected more often, being that she was surrounded by family. But then he thought that she had been dealt a pretty rough deal with Connor, and clearly couldn't see very far beyond that one insignificant person.

He'd actually been wondering, ever since he got back from Amsterdam, whether he was doing more harm than good where Hannah was concerned. Their lunch together made him question the hand that he'd had in trying to get her back together with Connor, as much of a failure as that had been. He wondered if the best thing to do as her friend would be to guide her back toward her husband and family. But then he'd spend time with her, and it felt so good to be with her that he rationalized that, despite no longer having the mission of bringing her back together with Connor, he himself was providing her with something she needed. He was her friend, and she needed a friend. He was giving her what she needed—right? Besides, it wasn't like he was *distracting* her from being a wife and mom—he was just making her time away from it more fun.

On Christmas Eve, Danny decided to give Akie a call overseas, to wish her a happy holiday, and to hopefully make arrangements to see her soon after the New Year. It would be Christmas Day in Tokyo. He dialed the number she had given him—it had been months since he had dialed it.   She answered the phone in her usual, low-key manner. Somehow it motivated him to an abundance of energy.   "Hey, Merry Christmas!   Long time, no speak!"   He really didn't know why he said such lame things when he called her.

"Thanks, Danny.   How are you?"

"Just spending the evening with my mom and some cousins.   What are you up to today?"

"Working," she said matter-of-factly.

"On Christmas?"   Danny was confused.

"Yeah, it's not a national holiday here.   And I'm not Christian, so, you know—I don't really miss it or anything."

Wow.   Danny realized just how little he knew about her.   They'd never really talked about religion at all, Danny being agnostic at best, but he had just assumed that everyone celebrated Christmas.   He decided to cover his blunder by changing the subject.   "That's cool.   So—you're gonna be Stateside soon, right?"

Akie gave a long pause.   "Yeah, uh—that's sorta changed.   It looks like they still need my guidance over here, so I'm hanging around another six months."

He tried not to sound as disappointed as he felt.   "Aw—you can't get out of it, huh?"

"I don't think I'd want to.   I'm learning a lot, and it's a great challenge to be a woman in a man's industry here.   It's kind of a rush, you know?   Doing something that a woman's not supposed to be able to do, and kicking the ass of all the men who tried."   She paused.   "I'm just not ready to come back yet, Danny—and…"   She trailed off.

He knew right away.   "You've met someone."

"Yeah—he's a pretty cool guy.   You'd probably really get along with him."   He could tell she was uncomfortable with the topic.   "Hey, how's the stuff with the band going?"

Danny tried to play up his enthusiasm. "Great—we have a big gig coming up at the Whiskey. Too bad you won't be able to see it!"

"What? Wow—yeah, too bad. But, hey, I'll look for a video on YouTube or something, okay?"

"Sure thing." Danny was sure that he didn't want to talk anymore. "Hey, I should probably get going, help my mom with some last-minute baking, you know? Call of duty."

"Totally! Hey, thanks for calling, Danny. And—Merry Christmas."

"You, too. Bye." He hung up the phone. He wasn't sure what he'd expected, but certainly not this. He shouldn't be surprised that Akie had found someone in Tokyo—after all, she was really hot. And he was fairly certain from the way she'd said it that it wasn't like she'd found the love of her life. More than likely, she'd probably just found someone new for a casual fuck here and there. But, still, he was bothered that it meant so much to him to have her return, and that it didn't seem to mean as much to her at all.

*

The Whiskey a Go-Go was legendary. It was considered by some to be the place that started the L.A. rock scene. The Doors had played there. Soundgarden had played there. And tonight, Danny was playing there. He was totally amped.

He had performed in smaller venues before, both with Montage and Exquisite Corpse, but never in any place of this significance. And this was the first time he was inviting his larger circle of friends and co-workers to a show. He hoped they would be impressed—especially Hannah. She had mentioned she was going to try to make it, and he couldn't help but be excited to see her. He knew she already saw him as someone special, but somehow it felt important for her to see him as he saw himself: not just a guy that worked in the office with her, with whom she'd shared some fun moments; but a serious musician with a serious talent. He couldn't explain why this meant so much—but it did. He hoped maybe he could steal a few minutes later with her, just the two of them. He must have had a distant look on his face as they carried the equipment onto the stage area, because Gavin nudged him.

"You thinking of the tiger or the M.I.L.F.?"

"Hmmm?"

Gavin gave a wicked smile. "Mmm-hmm. Must be the M.I.L.F. Will I get to meet her today? Or will she be traveling with husband in tow?"

Danny punched his friend on the arm. "Come on, Gav. She's not like that. And we're just friends."

Gavin snorted. "Uh, yeah. The last time you went out with your just friend you came into practice drunk and totally in your head. Not that I minded. You actually played a lot better. And I guess it's better than the chick that took your job from under your nose."

"Naw, man, Akie's cool, too. And I don't want you saying bad stuff about her, 'cause I really want to try to hook up with her again when she gets back from Japan."

"*If* she gets back." He gave Danny a pointed look. "In the meantime, I guess we're dealing with the M.I.L.F."

Danny laughed it off and continued to set up, but it made him think. Was he too focused on Hannah? And how *would* he act if she brought her husband? He hadn't thought of that before. It wasn't like they'd slept together or anything, but he had done some pretty intense flirting with her, and wondered if he could act casual if the guy did end up tagging along. Knowing about a husband was one thing—meeting the guy when you've been messing around in a way that wasn't altogether honorable was something entirely different.

He was waiting in the tech booth when he got her text.

"Lookin' good," it said.

He smiled, and then texted back. "Can you see me?"

"Yep," she replied. "Creepy, huh?"

He laughed at how straightforward she was, then glanced out among the venue, but he couldn't see her. "Super creepy. Where are you sitting?"

"With Tammy in the booths upstairs."

He breathed a sigh of relief. Hopefully, that meant she was without male companionship tonight. "Cool," he texted back.

"Good luck." There was a little heart typed next to it.

"Thanks," he replied, with a little winking face. He was ready.

He couldn't have hoped for a better performance, or a more welcoming crowd. Everyone they had ever known had shown up, it seemed, from co-workers to friends to long-lost acquaintances. Everyone seemed to want to share in this night. Danny rode a high that barely needed the multiple whiskeys he consumed, and he spent so much time greeting everyone that he had no chance to pull any one aside and have an intimate one-on-one. He didn't see Hannah until several friends had treated him, and could barely see straight when she approached.

She gave him an enthusiastic hug and spoke right in his ear. "Danny, you guys were amazing! I am so impressed!"

He beamed. "Thanks! Where have you been this whole time?"

"Oh, a bunch of us from the office were just hanging upstairs, away from the floor. And you've looked so busy we didn't want to interrupt you."

He gave her a look that said she should know better. "No worries. Where's Tammy?"

"She and her boyfriend went home. My husband's getting the car, so I actually have to go to the front and wait for him." The sense of dread that hit Danny at the mention of her husband was immediately calmed by the knowledge that he was no longer there.

"Awesome! Hey, Hannah—thanks for coming." He leaned over and gave her a sloppy hug, and a peck on the cheek. She responded by holding him maybe a little too long.

"Be safe getting home tonight, okay, Danny?" She finally let go, and looked back as she waved goodbye. He watched her leave, mixed emotions running through him. The first was pride that she'd finally seen him as the rock star he dreamed of being. The second was confusion. Why would she bring her husband tonight, to see him, when she knew that there was the possibility of being weirdness between all of them? Then, there was frustration, both at not being able to see her more, and also at knowing that it was probably best that he hadn't.

It was time to take a major step back.

*

Hannah arrived at work Monday morning, completely exhausted and in need of another weekend. Her husband and she had shared the most honest discussion they'd ever had, about their relationship and where they were going. In a way that was uniquely his, he had intuitively stated that he suspected that their intimate times together were not motivated by her feelings for him, and that it wasn't until they'd gone to Danny's show that he'd been able to put two and two together. She assured him that nothing beyond innocent flirting had occurred, and he believed her. But at the same time, he knew that he couldn't have a healthy relationship with someone who wasn't ready to fully commit to him. She had understood, and the whole discussion was very therapeutic. It had ended with them both agreeing to take the next obvious step.

She needed to get her mind off of things, so wandered to Danny's workspace. She wanted to congratulate him again on his triumphant night at the Whiskey. She knocked on the outer partition of his cubicle.

He turned around, and looked about as tired as she felt. "Hey, Mr. Rock Star."

. He beamed. "Hey! How are you?" He moved everything out of his guest chair so that she could sit, which she did.

"Tired. But so proud of you! That was so much fun on Saturday!"

Danny smiled. "Yeah, it was pretty amazing. We closed up the place, drinking with all the friends that wanted to treat us. They must have been glad to see us go."

Hannah smiled. Danny's existence was so very different than her own. "It must have been a high just to see that many people you know, all cheering you on."

"It was—and it wasn't just friends cheering. There were a few agents in the crowd. We may have a shot at something bigger because of this."

"Oh, Danny, that's wonderful! You deserve it!"

"Thanks!" He tapped her knee with his hand. "So how was the rest of your weekend? Spend time with the kids?"

Hannah sighed. "Somewhat…Do you have time for lunch today?"

He hesitated, a look that she couldn't quite interpret registering on his face. "Mmm, naw, I gotta buckle down on police station stuff."

"Oh." She looked down. There was an awkward silence.

"Everything okay?"

She shrugged and smiled. "Not really." She felt herself resorting to tears, and she really fought it this time so that they wouldn't come.

Something new registered in his face. He tapped her foot with his. "Hey, I could use some coffee. You wanna take a walk to the place on the corner?"

She smiled at him gratefully. "That sounds great."

They didn't say much until they got out onto the sidewalk in front of the building. Danny started. "So I talked to Akie when I was at my mom's."

Hannah forced a smile. "Oh, really—I didn't know that." It wasn't surprising. They'd not spent any time alone together since their last emotional lunch in December. Danny had gone home to visit his mother, and when he'd gotten back had been busy at work, not to mention band stuff. They'd only had time for one lunch together after a work conference, and then Elena and Eduardo had also been there.

"It hasn't really come up."

Hannah nodded. "I get it. How is she? Is she on her way back to the States soon?"

"Not anywhere close." She looked over at him, eyes wide. He laughed. "I guess she's not as eager to see me as I am to see her."

Hannah felt her emotions rising again. "Then she's a fool."

"I dunno. I think she does have feelings for me, I really do. She just doesn't want to commit. I guess I understand." He looked over at Hannah. "I've never been Mr. Commitment myself."

It stung to say what she said next. "But Akie makes you want to commit, where you never have before."

Danny nodded. "I don't understand why she doesn't feel the same way."

Hannah sighed. "I know what you mean. After everything that happened with Connor, I thought I could just pick things up with my husband, and I've been trying so hard to make it work with him."

Danny's brows furrowed. "Well, that's good, right? He's a good guy."

"He is—but he's also very intuitive. We've—been intimate a lot lately," she blushed, "But it isn't the same as it used to be. It's not him I'm thinking about, and he knows it." She looked over at Danny, hoping he'd get the clue, but nothing but cluelessness registered on his face. "He's moving out next month."

"What?" Danny was completely surprised. They arrived at the coffee place, and Danny opened the door for Hannah. As she passed through, he reached out to touch her arm. "Hannah, are you okay?"

"Let's order." They did, and once they were seated they picked back up on the conversation. Hannah started again. "I'm really at a loss for *what* to feel. On the one hand, I mean—the marriage that I have spent twelve years nurturing and growing is pretty much done. But then again, I guess I've felt it coming for a while, and I'm almost relieved that it's here, and playing out in a very respectable way. I mean, you know, we still have our kids, and we still love each other."

Danny nodded understandingly. "Are they okay?"

"They're fine. They don't really hear us fight. We haven't lately. It's all very calm and constructive conversation. We're just at the point where logic is setting in, and we're trying to figure out how the whole thing is going to work. There's the house, of course, and the question of how we're going to live in two places on the same income. We'll have to sell to afford two smaller places, but in the meantime he's looking for a cheap apartment with no lease. We're thinking he'll take the kids on weekdays, since he's always home at least three hours before I am. Then I'll take them over on weekends."

She paused to drink her tea. Danny looked unsure of what to say. "Geez, Hannah—I didn't know it had gotten so bad."

She shrugged. "It was never bad. It just—stopped working." She didn't want to tell him why it had stopped working. He clearly had no idea. "I'm just *not* looking forward to next month. I'm getting one year older, and I'm one step further from happiness."

"Your birthday's next month?" She nodded. "Well, that can't go uncelebrated. I may be kind of lost when it comes to comforting, but celebrating is my specialty. Let's celebrate you, Hannah."

She was touched that he wanted to help, in his own way. "I don't know, Danny…"

"I won't take no for an answer. We'll get the whole group together, and you can have a fun night out, get your mind off of all the heavy stuff. C'mon, pick a night. You deserve it." He put his coffee cup up, as if to toast.

Hannah smiled. She didn't need more confusion right now, but a happy hour with friends could not possibly lead to anything too crazy. She tapped his cup with her own.

*

Downtown Los Angeles was full of classy options for celebrating, but perhaps none more charming then the rooftop bar at Perch. Hannah had never been, and was excited to let her mind take a break from all of the heaviness in which she had been steeped. She, Danny, Tammy, Elena, and Eduardo all walked over from their office, anticipation building as the first elevator rose to the thirteenth floor. A second elevator delivered them to their destination, and a reserved table was waiting for them. They ordered a number of food items from the Happy Hour menu, but Hannah was so excited to be there (and near Danny) that she just couldn't set her stomach to eating much.

Drinking was easier—and did she ever drink. Everyone wanted to buy her a drink, and not everyone was going to be able to stay beyond a few hours. Hannah had taken to a one-drink-per-hour policy; but by the second hour and the fourth drink that policy had been all but forgotten. She was responding to conversations she barely heard, and laughing at snippets of jokes. Her head was swimming. And she felt no pain.

After the first two hours, Hannah decided she wanted to see the top floor, and excused herself for a few minutes to wander up the flight of stairs. Danny followed closely behind. She grabbed his hand, and leaned into him naturally. He didn't seem to mind. At the top, they looked upon Pershing Square together, and Hannah clung to Danny to shield herself from the February chill in the evening air. She gazed up at him, and he reminded her that they should probably return to the rest of the group.

The rest of the evening got especially hazy, until Eduardo had to leave, and the rest of them walked over to a corner coffee shop to sober up. It was as if Hannah started tuning in again. She could finally make sense of the words that were coming out of everyone's mouths, and realized she was clinging pretty heavily to Danny. She laid off a bit.

Elena looked at her watch. "Well, my husband's gonna have a cow if I don't get back soon. I still gotta walk back to the office."

"I'll walk with you," said Tammy. "I'm over there, too. You coming, Hannah?"

"You know, I parked at Pershing Square Garage this morning. I'm a planner like that."

Tammy laughed. "Didn't work out so well, did it?" Hannah shrugged.

"I'll walk you over there," offered Danny.

"Thanks!" said Hannah.

"Alright," said Tammy, grabbing her purse from the back of the café chair, "You two get home safely, okay?"

"We will," said Hannah, hugging her friend. She gave Elena a hug too, and waved them off. She turned to Danny. "Ready?"

"Yep." The two of them sauntered out the door.

Once outside, Hannah said, "Thanks for the idea of celebrating my birthday. I was kind of doubtful—but this made turning 37 worth it."

"Good."

"You know, I can drive you back to your car. I know you parked at the office. I guess I should have, too."

"You were planning well. The rest of us didn't. I don't mind."

Hannah smiled. "I liked Perch."

"Awesome place. You deserve it." Danny smiled over at her. His smile had the power to turn her stomach to jelly. They spent the rest of the short walk in relative silence.

After the two approached Hannah's car, she unlocked the drivers' side, while Danny waited to hold the door open for her. She turned to him again. "Thanks for an amazing night." She reached up and embraced him, kissing his jawline. He squeezed her in return, chuckling lightly, in his friendly Danny way. There, in his arms, Hannah realized that she wanted to kiss him. And she didn't want to miss this chance. It wasn't the most romantic spot—but then again, at the moment she didn't care. She pulled herself to his lips, and planted hers softly there. After a brief pause and a lazy glance into his eyes, she kissed him more aggressively, her lips opening to lock over his. It was perfect. She pulled away and looked up at him.

He was enchanted. "Let's get in the car," he said, and she quickly obliged as he sprinted to the passenger side. As each settled into their seats, they reached for the other in a synchronized haste, and began to explore the lush depths of their sealed mouths. Their tongues found a perfect rhythm, and it was as if they were both on the same beat of some unheard but intuitively sensed bassline. They separated for a moment, Danny taking a breath to say, "I knew you would be an amazing kisser." She beamed, and they plunged into each other's mouths again. Her tongue reached into his, searching and feeling. She ran one hand through his long and surprisingly soft hair, while she reached down with the other and rubbed lightly over the hardness in his pants. His hands squeezed around her sides, and down to her ass. She thought they would stop there, but he allowed one to delve under her skirt. In one move, his hand had pushed aside the seat of her panties (thank god she had worn the one pair of cute ones she owned, and not her cotton mommy undies), and his finger plunged into her wet and throbbing sheath.

She drew in a surprised breath at his reckless abandon. Wow—he skipped second base completely and went right for third. His finger wiggled around inexpertly as she continued to kiss him. She moaned. A few things were going through her mind at that moment. *God, he's an amazing kisser.* Then, *well, now I've gone farther with Danny than I ever went with Connor.* And, *Okay, when is he going to slow it down a bit so I can really feel things?* But that finger just kept wiggling around aimlessly. She tried not to think about it too much—she wanted to savor that amazing kiss without interruption, so the finger was just going to have to be tolerated. It wasn't like it was a bad feeling—but Hannah realized that, if she wasn't super-attracted to him physically and in the middle of the best kiss of her life, she would not be feeling anything Down Under, so to speak.

He really has no subtlety in his touch, she mused to herself, *But his kisses are perfect.*

They finally came up for air, and Danny withdrew his finger. He submerged it into his own mouth, sucking it clean. Wow—he must really like her. She wondered what it tasted like.

"Wow," she said breathlessly, taking him in. "Kissing you is like a dream come true." She realized her skirt was completely up, and that she didn't care. She was sure glad there was nobody else in the garage at that moment.

"I like your kitty underwear," he said mischievously. "Meow."

"I bet you do. You sure made yourself at home." She gave him a bedroom smile.

"That's just the beginning," he said, licking his lips.

She laughed. "I have to be honest with you. Cunnilingus really does nothing for me. It's all about the hand for me."

He raised an eyebrow. "Really?"

She shrugged. "It's called a PS-Spot. Kiss me again."

She didn't want to waste time talking, and she figured he'd do his homework later. And as he obliged her, with no more aimless fingering, Hannah was really able to focus on that perfect kiss, and she realized she wanted more. It was Danny that pulled away. "Hannah, you've got a long drive."

Hannah released a long, drawn-out sigh, looking at Danny's wrist-watch. She cupped her hand over the lump in his jeans and caressed. "I know. 9:30: I still have to pick up the kids from my husband's place."

He picked up her hand and kissed her fingertips. "Let's head out."

She drove him back to their office garage. Both traveled in relative silence. Hannah didn't know what Danny was thinking, but she knew what *she* was: she hoped this didn't end when Monday came around. She hoped that Danny wasn't another Connor.

*

They'd gone too far. And they hadn't gone far enough. These were the thoughts that battled in Danny's head the whole weekend. Up until they kissed, all Danny was really going for with Hannah was a friend-ship, maybe one where he could have some flirting fun, play out a little office fantasy. But her kiss really threw him off. He couldn't get her out of his mind.

And yet he knew he wasn't in love with her. Akie was the woman for him—he'd known that for a long time. She was his ideal: beautiful, voluptuous, powerful, and savvy. But Akie wasn't here, and hadn't been for a while. And Hannah was a warm, beautiful, sexy friend who kissed like no one he'd ever known. He'd spent the weekend imagining himself doing all sorts of graphic, X-rated things to her. Even cunnilingus, which he hoped she liked more than she had said. It was his best talent as a lover. Then he decided he'd better look up that PS-Spot so if what happened Friday happened again, he'd be ready. And then he'd tell himself that he shouldn't even go there, because Hannah was his friend and didn't deserve to be hurt again. Not by him, not by anyone.

So he'd convince himself to fantasize about Akie. He'd get a really good one going, and would decide to squeeze one out. And then Akie would morph into Hannah. He thought of the way she moaned, the way she tasted, the way she smelled, and he'd come hard. And then he'd feel guilty. It was a vicious cycle.

Hannah texted him near the end of the weekend, that she was missing time somewhere during Friday night, and was trying to find the receipt for the garage. Danny wondered just what portion of that evening the holes in her memory obscured. When Monday came around, Danny decided to try to be as cool as possible. He didn't know what he'd do if he mentioned their kiss and Hannah didn't remember. After all, she *had* been really drunk. So he thought it best to not say anything.

He laid low the entire morning, waiting for her to come to him. It was work, and there was plenty to get done without him laying wait in her cubicle like some eager fanboy. Besides, he didn't want her to perceive him as too desperate. It drove him mad how long it took her to stop by—he thought to himself that she must not have gotten as much out of that night as he did, and resolved that it was best for them to move on, anyway.

She peeked into his cubicle around 10:00. And she looked beautiful. He smiled at the very sight of her, and wondered to himself if he wasn't letting himself get too emotionally involved, after all.

"Hi, Danny!" she said brightly.

"Hey, what's up? Did you find that receipt?"

She gave a coy little smile and a wave of the hand. "Oh—yeah, I did. It helped a lot. I don't know why I was freaking out. I guess I just wanted to make sure I didn't forget anything." She raised an eyebrow and smiled wide. Then he knew she remembered, and that there were no regrets on her end. Relief flooded through his senses, and he realized that he was already pretty far gone.

He decided to just go with it. "Awesome night. Great place." He tapped her on the knee. She opened her legs a little wider in her seat. Wow—he really needed to be careful with her. It didn't take much to get her going, and she didn't seem to be ready to slow down much. And he'd been through these things enough to know that they needed to cool down, lest that fire between them burn out too soon.

"Hard to think of work when I still have that going through my mind," she said.

He laughed. "Well, you're gonna have to! We've still got plenty to do here, and it's only Monday. I've got tons of stuff to catch up on."

She looked a little deflated, but acquiesced. "Yeah, I guess you're right."

He let his toe reach out to hers. "And if we get enough done this week, we can reward ourselves with a nice, long lunch on Friday."

When they did go to lunch as promised, Danny made sure to keep it super-casual, a pizza joint in Little Tokyo. At one point, Hannah reached her lips up to kiss him, but he didn't allow himself to respond. It killed him to do it, but he had to slow her down. She was too good to let it all fizzle in a matter of weeks.

*

Hannah was only half-present as Tammy appraised the skinny jeans in the clearance section at Macy's. She'd been thinking a lot of Danny—in fact, he was pretty much a fixture in her head. Which made it all the more difficult when she was living the other 99% of her life. Nobody, not Tammy (with whom she'd spent the bulk of her lunches lately), not her best friend from high school, certainly not any of her family members, knew about what was going on. Everyone had been shocked by the divorce, and Hannah was constantly in the saving face zone where everyone was concerned. After all, she'd been with her husband for so long that the two of them had become like their own separate entity: one simply could not be viewed without the other. It made it somewhat easier to pass off her distant attitude: most of them probably just assumed that she was in shock from the dissolution of her marriage, and had no idea that her mind was constantly clouded by the memories of her stolen moments with Danny. The good thing about this was that no one gave a second thought to trying to fix her up with dates or anything, either. They understood that a proper mourning period should be observed—even if Hannah herself was secretly not observing it.

"I wish I wasn't so fat," said Tammy.

Hannah glanced at the tag on the skinny jeans her friend held. "Anyone that can wear a Size 7 cannot legally call themselves fat." She'd always considered her friend more robust or voluptuous—it was actually something she envied. Hannah had always felt almost too skinny to be sexy. She didn't have the boobs or the curves that made skinny on movie actresses so acceptable. She was just rail thin, with small breasts that had become non-existent after two pregnancies. Her legs looked like two sticks in skinny jeans. She was constantly in a state of wonder that Connor or Danny saw what they did in her at the age she was at— she hardly saw herself as any man's object of desire. Maybe that's why she was so fixated on keeping what she had with Danny alive. She didn't know if she could ever find anyone else that desired her the way he obviously did.

She returned her attention to Tammy, who was putting the skinny jeans back. "Size 7 is not so small when you're only 5-foot-2."

"Well, at least you have some curves to speak of—all I have is this super-luscious derriere." Hannah shook her bottom.

Tammy laughed. "Oh, brother. I should have such problems."

Hannah looked at the sales racks around them. "All that and you're not gonna get anything?"

Tammy hesitated. "I don't know." She picked the skinny jeans back up. "Maybe I'll just try them on."

Tammy ended up getting the skinny jeans, and by the time they'd purchased them and got a quick bite to eat an hour and a half had passed. The two rode back on the bus, ready to covertly return to the office. It was crowded because of the lunch hour, but they managed to find two seats right by each other. Tammy looked over at Hannah. "So I noticed you haven't been stopping by Danny's cubicle as much."

"Oh—really? I guess he's just been really busy with meetings on this police station project he's working on." Hannah hoped she was able to hide any disappointment she felt from her voice. "I do miss him, though."

Tammy raised an eyebrow. "Danny's cool. Just very self-absorbed."

Hannah smiled. "He's fun to have lunch with, though."

Tammy paused. "You two were doing that a lot for a while."

"We like the same kinds of places."

"You know, a lot of people at work have noticed. Dominic made a comment the other day about how our lunch group has been voted down to two. And he wasn't talking about you and me. And Elena asked me what was up between you two."

Hannah's heart stopped for a second. She'd really thought they'd kept under the radar this whole time. And now, what with how busy he'd been lately, she just assumed no one would give a second thought to their brief encounters in the hall or his cubicle. She thought for a split second of telling Tammy exactly what had been going on—but she knew Tammy would (rightfully) encourage her away from Danny. And Hannah wasn't ready to stop. "We're just friends."

"That's what I told Elena." Tammy gave a sidelong glance. "You know, I get wanting to hang around Danny. I really do. He's a hottie.

Just be careful, okay? You are really beautiful and really vulnerable right now. And I don't think someone with Danny's track record would give a second thought before taking advantage of that."

Hannah laughed, maybe a little too boisterously. "Oh, Tammy—I am not beautiful. And nothing's going to happen. I've got it completely under control."

"It's not about control, Hannah. Nature always wins. No matter what you say, you *are* beautiful, and Danny's a man. No amount of control can stop Nature. She always gets her way."

*

It was the end of March before the two were able to go out after work again. Danny swore it was because the band was trying to get a recording of their songs together, but Hannah was irritated that he didn't seem to be bursting inside the way she was. For weeks the only thing she could think of was his kiss, and his hands, and how much she wanted him to use them both all over her. And yet he gave no indication that he wanted to do any of that at all. She wondered if she'd been mistaken about what they felt, and whether to him there was nothing. He *had* intimated in past conversations that he'd lived that rock 'n' roll lifestyle—it probably meant a hefty share of one-night stands where a lot more than kissing was involved. She guessed she'd find out if she was more than "just one more" when they drank again. Booze was a great truth serum.

Their destination was a bar connected to a hotel in a so-so area of Downtown. She'd picked it for the photos she'd found online, of a dark room with red velvet sofas. Hannah knew that she wanted to sit in one of those sofas with Danny and do the sorts of things you're not supposed to do in a bar. And when she fantasized, she let it get to the point where they'd take it upstairs to the cheap hotel above.

She was ready this time. She'd bought a whole collection of cute underwear, and had made sure to wear a new pair every time they'd been out to lunch together. She was being extra conscious about personal grooming in her nether-region, too. The new cuts of underwear showed a lot more down there, and hair needed to be removed in the corresponding zones. She'd never had to think about these things back when she was married. And even before then, she'd been single in a world that had been pre-mainstream Brazilian wax. She'd read somewhere that young men now got most of their perception of female genitalia from easily-accessed online porn, in which the women were waxed clean. And even though Danny was her age, she'd bet that his latest conquests all went to the waxing salon with great frequency.

Problem was, even with all her preparation, Danny had provided absolutely no opportunity for her to show off her glossy new lower half. Every time they'd been out, they'd been painfully chaste, with only Hannah offering a peck on the lips. She would have liked for it to be more, but Danny never responded. It made her wonder why. She wondered if she'd have the nerve to ask him.

They left work early and drove together to the bar. Danny talked all the way, about the challenges he was encountering with the police station. She supposed anyone else would find it boring, but Hannah really appreciated the opportunity to talk to Danny about what he did. It had, after all, at one point been what she had dreamed of doing, and so it thrilled her to be able to speak to a like mind about it. He seemed to appreciate the chance to talk a little shop with someone willing. They parked in a lot a few blocks away from the bar and discussed marketing issues non-stop even as they ordered their first drinks and appetizers.

But as they moved into their second drinks, the talk diverted away from marketing strategies, and into more risqué ventures. Like when she got a berry-infused drink, and couldn't seem to get to the vodka at the bottom. She'd left that little bit for quite a while, until Danny noticed. "You can't already be giving up!"

She picked up the glass. "No, but I can't seem to get to that little bit at the bottom. That massive block of ice is getting in the way, and the berries are getting caught in the straw."

"Then suck harder," he said, placing his bourbon-relaxed hand on her thigh.

She turned to him. "I'd like to suck harder, but I haven't been given the chance lately."

He smiled, sticking his tongue out a bit. "You can practice a bit now."

"Gladly," she said seductively, plowing her mouth into his and allowing their tongues to engage in a mutual exploration. Her hand moved to his thigh, fingers brushing ever so slightly against his center of pleasure, and they allowed themselves to stay locked that way for a few minutes. They were only interrupted by the bar waitress, who discreetly took their order for more drinks.

Danny turned back to Hannah after the waitress walked away. "This is a lovely little vacation from real life. Thank you." He leaned over and kissed her, lightly biting her lower lip.

"Thank *you*. I'm having just as much fun as you are." She allowed her arms to reach around his neck, and crossed her leg over his, allowing it to rub freely against the lump it felt there. She hoped she was making him mad with want for her.

They downed the second drinks, which were very strong, quickly. Hannah was happily drunk, but not so much that she would black out and forget anything. Perfect drunk. She looked over at him, and he nodded. "Time to get you back to that train station?"

"Not quite," said Hannah, "But I don't mind if we have a little time to linger."

They made that their cue to pay the tab and exit the bar, arm in arm. A quick stroll and some chit-chat brought them to the parking structure. Danny opened the passenger door for Hannah, and then let himself into the drivers' side. The minute he did that, Hannah reached for him and they continued their intense kissing. When Danny came up for air, all he said way, "Back seat." He got up out of the car and opened the back door. Hannah simply climbed from the passenger seat into the back.

As soon as Danny sat down and closed the door, Hannah plowed her mouth onto his hard-on, which threatened to burst through his pants. She mouthed him intensely for a few minutes over his jeans, while he closed his eyes and enjoyed this sneak preview at the more that they could share. She looked up at him. "I wanna suck you dry." He grabbed into his pants and adjusted himself, then reached for her, so that she could straddle his lap. She allowed her mouth to explore his, and their tongues interplayed as if they both knew this favorite song. Hannah allowed herself to gyrate on top of Danny, and her strokes were as powerful as if he was inside of her. She was almost crazed with wishing that he could be.

Danny lifted her wiggle skirt up to her hips, and moved his hand under her cheetah-print panties, stroking her backside. He reached down from behind, for the area near her perennial, and started massaging, allowing his finger to creep into her wetness. "Is this the area you were talking about?"

"Yes," moaned Hannah in-between kisses. He was definitely in the right place, and although it felt better than his finger-play weeks before, she still didn't feel quite the same as when her husband or even she had done it before. So she simply decided to move their play into another position. She spun on top of him, skirt still up, and backed into him in a lap dance. She grabbed for his hand and stuffed it back into the front of her panties, allowing him to pet her while she intensified the gyration as she backed into him.

Danny groaned, and then lifted her off of him quickly. "I think I need some air." He quickly exited the back seat, and stood up next to the car, taking in a few deep breaths.

Hannah smiled. She might have made him almost pop right then and there. She felt a sense of pride that she could do so much to him, fully clothed. She wished she could do more. "Are you okay?" she asked, leaning out of the back seat to look at him.

Danny nodded. "Yeah, it was just getting a little hot back there." He got back into the car, sitting on Hannah's left, and she sidled up on top of him, allowing herself to be cradled there in his arms, skirt still up over her hips. He took the pony tail out of his hair and stroked her exposed thighs. She ran her fingers through his soft hair. He allowed his hand to settle over her damp panties. "Oh, man, you're soaking." He allowed his fingers to once again slip under her panties, and took a sample of the lubrication that threatened to ooze out. He rubbed his fingers over his lip, which he then licked. "This is more like it."

Hannah wondered if she'd been a little too aggressive with him. Maybe he wasn't used to a woman taking charge like that. "I wish we could go somewhere else."

Danny looked down at her. "Where? A hotel?"

Hannah nodded. "Yeah, but we don't have time. I have to get back to pick up the kids tonight. There's just no way—and this just feels so high school."

"Yeah. The back of my SUV is not the ideal place." He tilted his head back and gave a sigh. Then he looked down at her apologetically. "You're right. This is fucking high school." She traced his lips with her finger, and then reached up to kiss him. Once their lips parted, he let his eyes settle on hers. "Let's get you to that train station."

*

After putting the kids to bed later that night, with a burgeoning treasure chest of masturbation material and in the comfort of her own bed, Hannah explored the wonders of her own body. She shrugged her nighty off her shoulders and allowed her fingers to brush against the tips of her breasts. Imagining Danny was there hovering over her, she turned onto her stomach, and pulled her panties down below her derriere. She allowed her hand to explore from behind, imagining that sizable asset that she had only seen as a hump in his jeans had found its way between her legs. With two fingers softly pinching her nipples, and the other hand caressing her perennial sponge while the fingers brushed the outer edge of her labia, Hannah found the fulfillment that she hadn't gotten all night during her backseat playtime with Danny. As she rode wave after wave of orgasm, she allowed first one and then three fingers to enter the canal of her desire, where she was already overflowing with gratification. She imagined how deep the pleasure would be with that hard, thick cock staking its claim in her. One more powerful orgasm finished her off. She turned onto her back, spent and sustained, at least for the night.

Jesus. If only Danny could do *that* to her. She had to admit, her sex life was more exciting now that she had established herself as his playmate, although her soon-to-be-ex still won in the area of foreplay and sexual expertise. But her husband had not been the one that inspired her desire: it was Danny who she had running through her mind the whole time, Danny who sparked that tingle of need. If only Danny could touch her the way her husband once had; then she could actually be getting pleasure from fucking the man that made her sopping wet in the first place.

It was surprising that Danny had experienced so many encounters and yet had never learned the subtle nuances of pleasing a woman. Then again—that could be why he'd only ever been successful at one-night stands. Maybe that girl Akie had felt what Hannah felt; that he was just plain unskilled.

She thought back. Even her husband had to be taught—true, he was more of a natural, but it had gotten intensely better over time.

As realization hit her, Hannah shot up in her bed. "That's it!" she said aloud, before she realized that the kids were sleeping down the hallway. She stilled her body, listening, but they were sound asleep. Assured that all was well down the hall, she could focus once again on the dilemma with Danny. Hannah decided it was time to make a proposition.

*

Danny's head had been spinning since Friday. He couldn't believe how wild Hannah was. That lap dance she had given him had nearly made him burst in his pants. And he noticed that she'd groomed herself considerably more down there—all that was left was a silky veil of hair. He just didn't know how to resist her, even though he knew it would be wise to do just that. But when he thought of her laying there, in his arms, those pink cheetah panties the only thing between him and pure, wet pleasure, those soft thighs waiting to push against his hips, he swelled with need. Jesus, a man sworn to celibacy wouldn't be able to resist that—how did he think he could? He thought of her smile, and of her lips, her kiss, and of how hard he was, and he wanted nothing more than to see those lips wrapped around his cock as he choked her deep. What would those big, green eyes look like as they looked up at him from down below? How hard could he pull her soft blond hair as he commanded her to consume him? And would he be able to last long enough to plow it into her other end? Or would it end with his milky cum trickling out of the smiling corners of her obedient, rosy lips?

He remembered their agreement, and how she had promised that she was seeking nothing but fun from him. He wasn't so sure she still believed that, and he knew he couldn't commit to her in the way that she needed, for her kids and her happiness. No, it was best that they never take the foreplay into the full-fledged, hardcore sex that he imagined. He didn't think she was mentally ready for intimacy without commitment—and he was only ready for that with Akie. Friendship and fun—that had to be their rule.

When she entered his cubicle Monday morning, Hannah had a resolve he hadn't seen in her. She seemed so sure of herself. It was so hot.

"Wanna go to lunch again?" she asked.

Trying to keep his cool, Danny rolled back in his office chair. "On a Monday?"

Hannah laughed. "Come on, I've been waiting all weekend to see you."

Danny tried to be as aloof as possible. "Okay, but it can't take long."

"We can pick one of the quickie spots in the Arts District," resolved Hannah. "Besides, parking is free on that side of Downtown. See you at noon?"

Danny smiled at how determined she was. "Nooners it is."

"No, sweetie—just lunch," she said, and winked. He laughed. She sure did have a bit of the devil in her. It made her almost irresistible.

She was cool the whole way there. Not once did they talk about what happened last Friday at the bar—and after. Danny was starting to feel so at ease that he let his guard down. They talked about the final steps of getting the fire station built, and of some of Danny's plans for marketing the Grand Opening. It was like old times, and Danny wondered whether Hannah had realized how far they'd gotten and decided to pull back, too.

Once they got to the Arts District and found parking, though, she turned toward him, placing her hand on his thigh. "I thought about you all weekend," she said as she caressed it.

Danny laughed. "That's no fun."

Hannah let her hand move up. "Oh, but it was, Danny. I touched myself and thought of you. Of all the things I want you to do to me. I can't come anymore *without* thinking of you." She cupped his growing erection, and leaned over to kiss his neck.

"I've imagined doing a lot more to you, too. Many times." He let her continue to kiss and bite his neck. "I wish we could run away together, just ditch work one day."

Hannah took a break from her nibbling. "We could, you know. Just call me before I get off the train, and instead of taking the red line to work I'll take it to Hollywood, and we can have a fun day together." She settled back in the passenger seat. "Oh, Danny, why don't we?"

He looked at her regrettably. "Come on, Hannah. You remember our deal. We can't let this thing we have get in the way of our lives, and that includes our jobs. Our goals for success."

She looked at him. "And then there's that girl…"

"Akie," he said. It felt awkward to say her name at that moment. Hannah hesitated. "I'm sorry, Hannah—I think maybe that was insensitive."

"No—it's just that…"

Danny raised an eyebrow. "Just that what?"

Hannah took a deep breath before speaking. "What if I could guarantee you that the next time you see Akie, she will never want to leave again?"

Track 6

It had been a month since Hannah's proposal, and Easter was just around the corner. Danny wasn't religious or even Christian, but he still felt moved to practice Lent and give up Hannah for a while. Anyhow, it just worked out that way, too. At work, the fire station was over 75% completed and the Grand Opening had to be handled with special care. And there was no time to go out after hours, since Montage had begun recording their EP. All the interest from agents had to be responded to with a solid sampling of their music, and an intense week of laying down a few tracks to tape had been followed by weeks of careful mixing. It seemed that his dream of being a rock star was so close he could taste it. Sure, the name of the band sucked—no amount of subtle complaints from Danny had convinced the others to change it. But who cared? Once you were a success, no one cared about your name.

He was relieved to have the break from the complexity of his and Hannah's relationship. First of all, he wasn't sure if he wanted to have sex with her. What they had going on, as frustrating as it could be, was intense and exciting. Moving too quickly could put it all to an end. Second, this new mix of extreme intimacy and moral questionability had become heavier than he had been prepared for; it was getting less and less fun and more and more like work, having to weigh the pluses and minuses of their pairing. And, honestly, his ego had been somewhat bruised by her proposition. After all, she was implying that there was something that needed fixing, and no woman had ever told him that he was lacking in his lovemaking skills. He had never given them a chance to—until Akie. And the more he thought about it the more he wondered if that was why she had backed off in the first place.

Danny Ayres had never given a second thought to pleasing a woman. He had always taken what he wanted and moved on to the next, better conquest. It had simply never occurred to him that what he was doing was less than completely satisfying to them. It really wasn't until Akie that he had run into a woman that he had wanted again. Sure, there was Suzette, but she had been so obsessed with him that he wondered if she really had the self-respect to stop when it wasn't adding to her own pleasure. Akie was a woman who knew what she wanted and would settle for nothing less. When he thought back to their encounters, and compared them to what he'd felt so far with Hannah, he realized that she'd been pretty dry both times, and that it had been him that seemed to be having an out-of-body experience. He'd likened her lack of enthusiasm to her low-key personality or her preoccupation with her work—but what if it was that he just didn't know how to please her?

Come to think of it, he couldn't remember when he met a woman who got as moist as Hannah did. He always assumed that lubrication was a man's job, with his tongue and his pre-cum. He never imagined that a woman could be that damp with pure desire. It made him wonder if maybe she had a unique capacity to teach him what he never knew he needed to learn. Hannah had suggested they both get tested before her proposal could become a reality—he decided to swing by the clinic on his way home from work this week, just in case.

Hannah had been faithfully stopping by his cubicle every day, and Danny always completely dropped whatever he was doing when she showed. He wanted her to see that his intention was not to avoid her or ignore her—not even really to keep her at arms' length. Just to buy him some time before their next encounter alone together. It was more of a healthy break. He'd noticed that she'd been hanging a lot with Tammy lately—probably good for her to get some girl-time in.

When she settled into his guest chair on Good Friday, he knew something was up. She'd seemed to retain her bright and carefree attitude this whole time, but today she looked dejected. "Tammy put in her two-week notice."

Danny raised his eyebrows. "What?"

"It's actually a really great thing for her. She's been thinking of becoming a nurse, and she applied to a really competitive program. She got in over hundreds of others."

"Wow—good for her." Hannah's eyes started to fill with tears. "Whoa, Hannah—what's wrong?"

Hannah brushed away the tears with her forefinger. "It's just—she's the only friend I have who wants to spend any time with me anymore."

"What? Hannah—it's the opposite. Everyone wants to spend time with you."

"Not really. Not like Tammy. I mean, Elena's cool but she's just so busy all of the time. And you never want to spend time with me anymore."

"Hannah, that's not true. You know I've just been super-busy with work and the band. It is not about you. And you and Tammy are always together, so I think other people would like to spend time with you but maybe don't know that you have any time for them."

The tears were streaming now. "When Tammy's gone, I just feel like I'm going to be all alone. Everything's changing."

Danny put a soft hand on Hannah's knee. "Aw, Hannah…things change. You can't avoid that. But that doesn't mean you are alone. I am always here for you—I promise. Friends to the end."

Hannah laughed, in spite of herself. "You're really not avoiding me?"

"Hannah, I'm right here! Does this look like avoiding? If I was trying to avoid you I'd crawl under my desk until you were gone." Hannah laughed again. "Look, in a few weeks the mixing on our EP should be done. That works out perfectly for you and me to throw Tammy one more, big happy hour bash. We'll make it a special one."

Hannah beamed. "I have been wanting to check out that bar at Hotel Fig…"

"Bam, let's do it!"

Hannah got up out of the chair and draped herself over Danny. He felt like his heart would melt. "Thank you, Danny. You always know how to make me feel better."

He squeezed her in return. "I don't like to see you sad."

She kissed his neck. "Stay in my life and I won't ever be." She moved to the opening of his cubicle. "I'm going to go talk to Tammy about whether a Thursday night will work for the happy hour. See you later!"

"All right." Danny looked at the empty space she'd left after she'd gone. He wasn't sure how the future was going to work out, between Hannah's proposal and Akie still being his number one desire. But he wouldn't worry about that for now. He'd just look forward to the happy hour, and be sure to leave the negative test results in his wallet.

*

Danny checked the rear view mirror one more time before getting out of his car. His temples seemed much greyer than they had been only one month before. But, then again, he was 37 years old—38 in two months. Time was definitely not on his side. It was strange how this newest sign of age had set him into a sense of urgency: like the decisions he made needed to fit into part of the bigger plan for his life. The time for fucking around was seriously drawing to a close. It was almost like there was a shelf life to his youth—and he'd hit it.

He resolved not to expect anything from tonight. Hannah hadn't mentioned her proposal since the day she'd made it. And he'd sort of been avoiding opportunities for her to bring it back up. Because if she brought it up, Danny would be the one obliged to make a decision. And he got the feeling that his ability to resist was fading with the brown in his hair. He knew that when Hannah and he got drunk together lately, a lot more than just flirting had happened. And he couldn't help hoping that something would happen, something big. He had a sense this was his last chance for a fling—for something fun and carefree. He could feel the gravity of his existence weighing heavily—that beyond Hannah was an unavoidable change on the horizon. Everything after this would have to mean a whole lot more.

Hannah and Tammy were walking from the other direction when he saw them. They all stopped at the front door of the Hotel Figueroa. "Just us?" he asked "Everyone going home to watch the Kings win?" He couldn't help but notice how hot Hannah looked, in a light and scarf-like skirt and tight, plunging button-up cardigan.

"Nope," said Hannah, "Eduardo's on his way, Elena can stop in for one drink, and Dominic and his sister will spend a few hours before some big birthday party they're going to."

"Cool—let's get inside and stake a claim."

Once they'd walked past the hotel lobby and to the bar inside, they realized that staking a claim was hardly necessary. The place was empty, except for the bartender, who greeted them with a smile. They ordered some drinks and took the place in. On one side of the bar was a bed covered in mosquito netting. For a split second Danny considered claiming that spot—but then he thought the better of it and went with the girls to a poolside table.

"Not much going on here tonight, is there?" asked Tammy.

Hannah looked around at the colorful lighting and the turquoise pool, surrounded by trees. "No T.V. to watch the game. I'm sorta glad about that. It's just nice and chill."

A voice came up behind her. "Give us a few moments, and we'll fix that in no time." Dominic settled next to Tammy, and his sister in the seat next to him.

Soon Eduardo and Elena arrived, and the group were soon done with their first round of drinks. Eduardo bought the next round in Tammy's honor, and by the third round everyone was feeling pretty relaxed.

Dominic looked at Hannah, a gleam in his eye. "Hey, Hannah—you should jump in the pool!"

Hannah shook her head. "Um, no—I don't have a swimsuit."

"Who needs a swimsuit?" joked Tammy. "I think someone needs to take a dunk—Dominic, grab her arms and I'll grab her feet." She winked as she said it.

Hannah squealed, and scooted into Danny's lap. "Danny, don't let them get me!" She buried her face in his neck.

"I got your back, girl!" He let his arm encircle her waist, and for the rest of the night she stayed in his lap. Everyone else was so drunk they didn't ask questions as to why. And if they noticed Hannah nibbling at Danny's ear, they didn't say anything.

The group thinned slightly when Elena and then Eduardo left, and a little after 9:00 Tammy looked at her watch. "Alright, guys, I hate to be the party pooper, but I've got a long drive ahead of me. I think I'm gonna call it a night."

Dominic looked at his phone. "Yeah, we should probably get to that birthday party now. I think we're late enough to be stylish."

"Are any of you still parked at the office? Hannah and I walked over," explained Tammy.

"I actually parked my minivan in a funky lot this morning, east of L.A. Live," said Hannah. When everyone looked at her like she was crazy, she shrugged. "I only had a few bucks on me, and it's cheaper over there. I don't have office parking like you all do, not with public transit."

Dominic shook his head. "I'm still over there, Tammy. We can walk together."

Danny looked at Hannah. "I'm parked in the lot just around the corner. I'll drive you to your car." They all made their way to the front of the hotel and said their goodbyes. Hannah and Tammy shared a long embrace, and then Tammy moved toward Dominic and his sister, heading north, and Hannah walked with Danny to the south. Once they cleared the corner, Danny grabbed for Hannah. He'd enjoyed feeling her soft bottom rubbing against his lap, and he didn't want her far from him now that she'd been near the whole night.

She looked up at him, beaming. "What a fun night! I'm glad we could send Tammy off in style."

Danny squeezed around Hannah's waist. "Me, too. Another awesome spot you picked." They continued walking toward his SUV, which was deep in an open lot. Once inside the car, Danny turned to Hannah. "I want you to hear something. It's a rough mix, but I think you'll like it." He turned the key to auxiliary power, and got out an unlabeled CD from the console. He advanced it to his favorite track.

When the music started, Hannah nodded her head. "This is a rough mix? Sounds pretty good to me!" She turned to Danny. "I can tell you worked really hard on it, Danny. Congratulations." She leaned over and started to kiss him. Danny returned her kisses hungrily, feeling invincible with his music blasting and the alcohol running through his veins. He reached his hand under her skirt, and started kneading at the ass that had been inadvertently tempting him all night. Hannah responded by mounting him right there in the driver's seat, and she rocked her lower body against his, almost perfectly in sync to the music. Danny's hard-on throbbed.

Hannah separated her lips from his long enough to moan, "Oh, Danny—I want you so bad. When are we going to fuck?"

Her saying that word just made him harder. "Hannah, I want you, too—but not here. Not like this. Not in a car."

Hannah collapsed off of his lap. "Did you get tested?"

Danny reached into his pocket and took out the folded test results. He unfolded it and showed it to her by the light of the parking lot lampposts. Hannah looked it over and then smiled. She grabbed a similar paper out of her purse and showed it to him. Then, she took the paper from his hands, re-folded it, and then moved to stuff it back into his pocket. She then moved her fingers to the button of his pants, undoing it despite the awkward position, then unzipping them slowly. She allowed her hands to reach into his briefs and reveal the tip of his fully erect stalk. Smiling with bedroom eyes, she moved her head down and brushed her lips around the tip, allowing her tongue to brush it, ever so softly. She looked back up at him.

Wordlessly, he stuffed himself back into his pants, fastened them, and turned off the car. He got out and opened her door for her, offering his hand. Hannah obligingly took it, and they walked quickly back to the hotel, where Danny signed for a room while Hannah waited by the elevators. Once checked in, he grabbed her hand and led her into the elevator. His fingers wound tightly around hers as they waited in anticipation for the elevator to stop at their floor. He pulled her toward the room with more desperation than he could remember feeling in a long time. After fumbling with the key, he finally got the door open, and ushered Hannah in before him. Once they were both inside, he reached for her and started kissing her hungrily. Looking up to get his bearings, he backed her into the room, and onto the bed, where she plopped down, looking up at him.

He quickly undid his pants and pushed them down and off his legs. Without command or hesitation, Hannah grabbed for his protruding member, leaned down, and started to suck deeply and hungrily. Danny thought his head would spin off its neck for how good it felt. As she sucked, Hannah moaned with pleasure, just the way he'd seen in porn movies but had never experienced in real life. He didn't know that real women could love sucking cock that much, and couldn't believe his luck. She brought her legs up so that she was laying on the bed, grabbing a pillow with a free arm to place under her neck, and Danny allowed his knees to settle against the side. It was a rather high bed and so allowed for this sort of creative romp; lips still locked around his penis, Hannah pulled her skirt up, and Danny reached his hand down under her panties to caress her soft, wet pussy. He tried to lose his finger under her sheath, but she turned over on her knees, waist still bent in a yoga-like pose so that she could continue his oral pleasure, and started to pull her panties down. Taking the hint, he helped her, settling his hand between her thighs, caressing her from behind. She gently guided his hand to massage her perennial area, not allowing his fingers to enter her canal, but guiding his hand to relax and cup her whole vaginal area, as if it were a priceless treasure. She separated his fingers and allowed them to gently brush the outer edge of her labia as he stroked her slowly and methodically. After he did this for a few minutes, her moans got louder.

"Fuck, yeah," he whispered.

Hannah looked up at him and stopped sucking. "Let's save some for me." She straightened her body, standing and facing him, and unbuttoned her cardigan. Her bra was one of those ones with a front clasp, and soon her small but perky breasts were shining in the moonlight. Danny reached up to fondle one roughly, his fingers pinching them eagerly. "Softly," she whispered, and guided his hand to a gentler touch. "It is one of my most sensitive erogenous zones, so a little goes a very long way." Danny caressed one nipple lightly, and dove his head down to mouth the other, biting it delicately while his tongue rubbed it.

Hannah moaned with pleasure, reaching for his other hand. "Rub my back." She placed it right at the base of her back, and after a few more minutes moaned, "I want it from behind."

She turned back on her knees after climbing back onto the bed and placed her meaty backside against him, pulling his cock between her legs. As he rubbed up against her, she held his cock firm against her clitoris with one hand, while she placed her weight on the other. He realized what she wanted, and made sure to stroke fully so that he was rubbing her perennial and clitoris simultaneously. "Oh, God," she moaned, and he reached around with both hands to play with her nipples while continuing his purposeful gyrating. She got even wetter than before, and he thought he'd go crazy if he couldn't puncture her soon. But he knew what she was waiting for, and continued to rub up against her vaginal area from behind without penetrating. Her body started to tense, and he realized that she was starting to orgasm.

"Now!" she commanded, and he obligingly plowed his rod into her waiting sheath. They cried out in unison. She was tight and wet at the same time, and he could feel the friction he was creating as he moved in and out of her. He instinctively sped up, but she reached behind and held his hips. "Slowly, still. I have a few more in me." He enacted the discipline of a great athlete to methodically and fully stroke her, until he could feel her body tense in a second and then a third intense orgasm. Once her body relaxed the third time, she grunted, "You can fuck me as hard as you want now."

Without hesitation, Danny pulled her hair as he had fantasized, and started to ram her with everything he had. "Oh, Hannah," he called out huskily.

"Don't hold back, Danny! Pull my hair! Fuck me hard! I need it hard!"

"Whatever you want," he said, and he pulled harder on her hair, so that her back arched, and he held her hips as he continued to plow into her. The bed shook, and a rhythmic smacking sound resonated in the room every time he slammed into her from behind. He finally exclaimed, "I think I'm gonna come!" Hannah nodded.

He came harder than he ever had in his life—it was like his whole body released the warm fluid he injected her with. He didn't realize it was possible to come like that. He shook with relief as they collapsed on the bed together, and he could tell she was shaking, too. They lay there for some time, shallow breathing in sync and bodies hot from their intense workout. As he kissed the back of her neck, he wondered why he'd waited so long to take Hannah up on her proposal. He never realized just how much he'd been missing by waiting to sleep with her. And it was more than just the physical rapture. Fucking Hannah was like a drug that transported him to a different plane of existence, a plane that was exclusively theirs, one where his mind was clear of the past or the future. He hadn't thought of Akie once tonight, nor had he missed her like he had been lately. This realization settled in as he dozed off to sleep, and he could feel Hannah doing the same.

They woke from their little cat nap with a start. "What time is it?" asked Hannah, and she kissed him fully on the lips before getting up and hastily making her way to the bathroom. When she emerged, she had re-fastened her bra and cardigan. Her skirt had been on the whole time. She turned the light on for the first time since they'd arrived in the room, then grabbed for her underwear and shimmied back into them. She looked around as she did so. "Wow, too bad we can't keep enjoying this place. It's beautiful in here."

Danny was still laying down with his bottom half completely exposed. He looked around at the warmly painted walls and Middle Eastern accents. The setting screamed sex. "Don't you want to stay the whole night? I'll bet there's more in me where that came from."

Hannah giggled. "I'm sure there is, but it's almost midnight. I told my ex that I'd be late to pick up the kids, but this is hedging into the ridiculous. The little one'll probably be asleep by the time I get over there."

Danny forced himself up from his resting position. "I don't want you to fall asleep on the way home. Will you be okay?"

Hannah smiled. "Men get sleepier after sex than women. You have no idea how energized I am right now, Danny. I could run a few laps. And I don't like running."

Danny laughed. "Well, I think I'll stay here for the night. But I'll walk you out to your car. Where did you park again?" He grabbed his pants from the floor and started to shrug them back on.

"Far," said Hannah. "The walk just might wake you enough to give you the energy to get back to the Westside."

"Doubtful," said Danny with a mischievous smile, "but maybe I'll find some hot Kings fan who's ready to celebrate and make the room worth the money I paid." Hannah smacked him on the arm. "Kidding!"

"She'd never compare to me anyway," said Hannah haughtily.

Danny grabbed for her. "That," he said as he kissed her hungrily, "is very true."

They walked lazily to the parking lot, and it was far. But Danny was glad for the time with Hannah. He was sorry that he wouldn't see her again until Monday, what with this being a long weekend for the both of them, but that just seemed to be how their relationship played out. The week*days* were theirs, but the week*ends* belonged to the lives they had made before they had met—the lives that took up most of their non-working hours. The two never seemed to merge. He wondered if they ever could; but then he thought that there was no way he could be a family man at this point in his life, and he knew that her life had to be for her kids. The separation was there because it worked.

The drug he'd consumed was wearing off—the past and the future were creeping back in. He had to remember to keep himself lodged in reality, for both of their sakes.

*

Hannah spent the weekend absentmindedly managing her son and daughter while uncontrollably re-playing the encounter she'd shared with Danny. It was like a track on repeat, playing in the background of her mind ad nauseam. She knew that she wanted him, but had never imagined that the two could share such a raw, hardcore lovemaking session. It was like another version of Hannah had inhabited her body and screamed all those illicit commands. It wasn't unsettling or even unfamiliar; it was just a part of herself that she'd only ever allowed to perform in her head. Having Danny see it was strangely empowering— like she should feel some sort of shame because of what society expected of a 37-year-old mother of two, and consciously refused to. She had texted Danny when she'd gotten to her ex's place to pick up the children, and he replied what a great time he'd had. His texts were always unsettlingly vanilla. She hoped he wasn't off-put by her taking charge of their lovemaking like that—he hadn't seemed to be at the time. Still, she wasn't sure what to expect when she saw him again on Monday.

The more Hannah re-played the scene in her head, the more she was taken by the strange contradictions it encompassed. On the one hand, she now could say she knew Danny intimately, and that he had seen an unrated side of her that no one else had; on the other, since the lights had been off the whole time and all but her undies had remained on her body, albeit unfastened or pulled up, he hadn't really physically seen her at all—just little portions. And even though she felt like she was starting to understand his body and how it worked, she had really only seen his lower half—his shirt had stayed on the whole time. It was as if these coverings they had retained allowed that veil of mystery to remain between them; it was strangely arousing to have someone in a manner that was covert and somewhat clandestine.

She came to an odd realization in her head: there was a world that she was a part of, one where she was a lover and an object of desire. And nobody but she and Danny knew that she was a part of it. It made it all the more mystical—if either one ceased to remember would that world still exist? Part of her wanted to tell somebody, just to tether that world to some manner of reality—but Tammy was the only one she could imagine telling. And Tammy wouldn't be there on Monday. Then she realized that was probably a good thing, because the moment she disclosed what had occurred would be the moment it would cease to be magic; it would instead become a potential incident for doubt and shame. Hannah knew she didn't want that to happen.

As it was, her ex's usually understanding manner had been pushed to its limit last Thursday night. He didn't shout or even condemn; he just shook his head as he lifted their sleeping 7-year old into Hannah's van, as she guided the drowsy 9-year-old inside. Once they'd gotten the kids inside, she'd thanked him.

Cautiously, he started to speak. "Look, Hannah, I know this divorce has been difficult for you. It's been pretty rough for me, too. And I know you're really struggling to figure out who you are now. But I really need you to try to be on it with the kids. You knew I have a business trip coming up, and that I fly out tomorrow. I don't mind that it ran a little over, but a text or a phone call would've been nice."

Hannah had apologized profusely, and they'd left on good terms, but she knew that a change needed to be made to how she and Danny managed their relationship. They continued to count on inebriation to springboard them into intimacy; it was like being on a persistent one-night stand. Why did they have to act so coy with each other, if they'd already broken the wall between the platonic and the sexual? Why did it have to be a secret now? Sure, the clandestine thing was a high, but they could do that with another level of consciousness still at play. The mystical didn't have to depend on alcohol, did it? She hoped she'd have enough courage to raise this question with Danny soon.

Hannah took extra care to dress flatteringly Monday morning. She wore a charming little lacy pink dress with a skinny brown belt and her brown sandals, and made sure that her hair was perfectly in place. If she was living in a fantasy and sought to ease it back into reality, then she certainly didn't want her image to betray anything less than fantastic.

Although obscurely-understood rules for dating seemed to expect her to be less eager when she got to the office, Hannah found herself ignoring those expectations, and instead listened carefully for Danny's arrival in the still-quiet office. He was usually pretty covert, but some-times he'd greet a few people walking in. When she heard nothing, she turned to her computer to see if his green dot would show up in chat. Once she saw that it did, Hannah walked eagerly toward his workspace. Before she could get there, Dominic emerged from his cubicle, which was just two spaces from Danny's.

"Esther Williams, as I live and breathe! Oh, my, honey—did you make it to your car okay? We were worried that you were going to have to summon your inner Survivorman with how far it was!" He winked.

Hannah laughed, despite her nervousness at being seen entering Danny's work area, like somehow people in the office would make even more of it than they had before, now that there was a large degree of truth to the rumors. "Danny escorted me nobly to my far-off chariot, sweetie—thanks. How was your party?" She saw Danny emerge from his cubicle at the sound of her voice, and she tried to give as casual and friendly a wave as possible, lest Dominic catch on to some resonant intimacy vibe between the two of them.

"Oh, more drinking, more debauchery. I'm telling you, honey, you should've taken a dive into that pool. You can't know how fun it is to loosen up every once in a while."

Danny leaned against the inner opening of his cubicle, an amused gleam in his eyes. "Not Hannah—she's too much of a by-the-book kinda gal. And that's lucky for us, Dominic. She keeps us honest."

Hannah smiled, and used that as an excuse advance toward him. "Someone needs to!"

"Beauty is wasted on the straight-laced," said Dominic ruefully. "I'm off to my meeting—toodles, kiddies!" He turned to walk toward the end of the aisle.

Danny looked after him, and then as soon as he turned the corner grasped at Hannah's belt. He used it to pull her into his cubicle and into his arms, reaching around her backside to feel her up over her clothes. His voice remained casual. "You know, if that sort of thing had happened I'd ask when you were gonna give a repeat performance." He grabbed her hand and pressed it against an already fully developed erection.

Hannah tried to hide the shaking in her voice that threatened to surface from her pure relief at having Danny greet her so warmly. "Well, there'll be no nighttime performances this week, unfortunately. Looks like my nightlife will consist of the Disney channel and homework for the time being." She got up on her tiptoes to kiss his neck quietly. "But I'm open for lunch if you're game."

"Totally!" He ran his hand over the lace that covered her breasts.

She closed her eyes with anticipation. "Great—I'll chat you when I'm ready to go."

Danny raised his eyebrows. "I'm ready to go now."

Hannah laughed. "We just got here! Good things come to those who wait."

Hannah couldn't wait very long, though, and at 11:00 she sum-
moned him via instant message to meet her in the downstairs lobby. He
came down just a few minutes after she did, and they walked to his car,
side by side but not touching. There was just too much risk of being
seen. Danny looked down at Hannah. "Any ideas for where to go?"

"Arts District?"

"Cool." She'd picked the Arts District because it was close enough
so that they could get there quickly, but far enough so that she knew no
one else from their office would be anywhere near. They drove out
across Alameda Street, and Hannah led him to park in a far-off and
isolated side street surrounded by semi-abandoned industrial buildings.
There was no one walking around. The two made the considerable hike
to the more happening part of the neighborhood and had a quick lunch
at Wurstküche, where Danny told Hannah all about his weekend of final
mixing on the EP. She was excited for him to be so close to another
chance to show what he could do, musically. They talked nonstop.

But the talking stopped as soon as they got back to the SUV. They
had fulfilled their obligation to eat, and now could wait no longer to
share another taste of what amazing flavors they could create together.
Intense and starving, they devoured each other like they had devoured
the sausages and beer just a few minutes before. Danny pulled away
from Hannah, and stuck his finger in her mouth. She started sucking it
suggestively. "Tastes like sausage."

"I've got another one I want you to taste," he murmured.

Hannah looked around where they were parked. She hadn't seen a
soul walk past when they'd left the car to go to the restaurant, and
hadn't seen anyone around the whole time they'd been kissing. He
frantically unbuttoned his pants and revealed the erection she'd felt
earlier at his desk. The sight of it made her hungry, and she dove her
head down to consume it to the back of her throat. She couldn't suck
hard enough, so deep was her desire. She heard him breathing shallow-

ly; she wanted to tease him relentlessly. She could feel from the way his body tensed that her suckling was having the desired effect, and it thrilled her to be doing this to him in the middle of the day, on a public street, in the middle of a work day. She started to come without him even touching her. She released his cock from the cocoon she had formed with her mouth. "I need you right now, Danny." Waiting for no invitation, she mounted him where he sat, hastily pushing her panties out of the way. Her throbbing opening enveloped him with a slam, and she allowed herself to pound against him with a violent passion she could not control.

"You are incredible," he uttered breathlessly.

She allowed herself to cry out when she orgasmed, and could feel that he had, too, as she collapsed against him. It was fortunate, since she didn't have any paper towels handy to catch whatever came trickling out—their coming at the same time would buy her a little time before she would need to tend to business. She supposed it was the advantage to using a condom—but between their mutual negative test results and her religious use of the pill, she had made the conscious decision to take the risk involved with feeling everything one's lover had.

"Jesus," he said, "We have got to find a way to grab some time together that's not in the car. As much as I love the spontaneity of this little romp, all we need is to see one person that recognizes us before we start having some serious issues."

"My ex is out of town. It's just me with the kids for a little while. There's no way we can do anything after hours, and it seems silly to get a hotel room for lunch only."

Danny nodded. "It feels pretty seedy, too. Okay—we'll have to figure something out."

Hannah realized, despite their consumption of beer just a few minutes before, now was the time to make a case for a more lucid relationship. "Danny, why don't we run away like we talked about before? You know, go to the beach for a day instead of work? Take a walk on the pier? Give ourselves just a little chance to experience what it's like to not have to hurry back?"

Danny shook his head. "Hannah, you know we can't do that right now, not with the fire station at this critical point. We both gotta be completely present at work. Your kids need you to bring home a paycheck, and you can't do that if you're putting projects at risk because we wanna have a free day."

He made a good point—he always made a good point. "I know—it's just that I am really enjoying where we've been going with our relationship..."

"Me, too—Hannah, the sex is really amazing. You promised to train me all up so I'd be primed and ready to go next time I get a shot with Akie." Hearing that name stung Hannah deeply in her heart. "I really appreciate this Sensei/pupil thing we've got going on—there's not many women who would do that for someone else. That's already sacrifice enough. I don't want you to sacrifice your integrity as a Civil Servant, too."

Hannah wanted to cry. But she couldn't be angry at Danny. After all, that was how she'd framed her proposal for intimacy in the first place. It was a means to an end—an end that didn't involve her. She forced herself to nod her head. "You're right, Danny—we'll figure out a better solution. Let's dive back into the work pool, Esther Williams style."

And dive back in they did. Hannah saw Danny a lot during the rest of the week, because planning and meetings for the Grand Opening were intensifying. But there were no opportunities to get away for lunch, and they parted on Friday in a strangely professional manner. Eduardo had called them both into his office, and the spur-of-the-moment strategic planning session had lasted until day's end. Hannah had to assert that she couldn't be late for her train, because she had to pick up the kids from daycare. So Eduardo had waved her off, asking Danny to stick around for a few more minutes. There would be no chance at a secret little goodbye, like they had been doing every day that week in his cubicle.

As the train carried her homebound, Hannah felt a little buzz on her phone. She looked down—it was a text from Danny. "Still coming up with ideas for better lunches. ;) Have an awesome weekend!"

She looked up from her phone and sighed. There was no getting around it. She was falling in love with Danny. She'd done it on purpose, to forget Connor, but now she was finding it difficult to control. And she needed to control it. Because, as much as she knew he might care for her in his way, she was sure that Danny didn't love her. Not like that. He saw her as a work friend, one with definite benefits, but not one that he wanted to blend into his regular existence. Sure, the weekends were impossible because of her custody schedule with the kids; but the two shared the same regular day off every other Friday. Despite that, he had never proposed seeing her on days that he wasn't already in Downtown. She knew that what they had was there because it was convenient for him.

But just because he doesn't feel that way now, doesn't mean that he can't come to feel that way in the future, she thought. Maybe their sexual chemistry would get him so hooked that he'd forget about Akie and eventually want to be with her. The logical, earthbound part of her mind told her not to hold her breath. But the part that resided in that special, mystical place exclusive to her and Danny hoped that it might be so.

*

Danny had an idea. He chatted Hannah first thing on Monday to meet him in the downstairs lobby at 11:00 sharp. Once he got her response, he hurried to a meeting for the police station. It was a long, boring meeting, one that he probably didn't need to be at. The only thing that kept him going was the key that he felt imprint on his thigh in his pocket. Hannah would be pleased.

He hurried to the elevator lobby the minute he got out of the meeting. Hannah was already waiting. She looked amazing in an old-fashioned looking red shirtdress. "Danny, what's going on? You look like the town gossip that's just been told a secret."

He chuckled. "Something like that. Come on." He waved his chin towards the parking lot. The drive didn't take long, only about 10 minutes. They parked in a funky street next to an unassuming beige building.

"Is this some new lunch place you heard about?" Hannah looked completely confused.

"It's better than that," said Danny. He opened her door for her and led her towards the studio-style building. He stopped her in front of a door, and used the key to open it. He ushered her in, though she looked hesitant to enter. "It's okay, it's our band's rehearsal space."

She looked at him dubiously, but walked in, and Danny followed, closing the door behind them and turning on the lights. They were greeted by a small space, filled with a drumset, guitars, some amps, a sofa, and not much more. Hannah turned to Danny. "Okay, I'll bite. Are you going to play me a song or something? Did I finally inspire you to write that masterpiece?"

Danny laughed. "Not quite. Just have a seat." Obligingly, Hannah plopped onto the sofa, and Danny settled down next to her. He pulled her skirt up and started to rub her thigh. "It's better than the car, right?"

Hannah looked at him like he was crazy. "In your band's rehearsal space, Danny? I don't know—it feels awfully intrusive. I'd feel awkward. This is supposed to be for you and your bandmates, not us."

Danny moved his hand up to unbutton the top two buttons of her shirtdress. He tugged her bra down to reveal her perky breasts and started to play with the nipples, just the way she had shown him at the hotel. "Your body appears to disagree." He kept one hand at her breasts, then moved the other down to caress under her panties. Breathing heavily, she arched her back and clawed at his pants. He quickly unzipped them, exposing himself. "We can just play."

Taking him up on his invitation, Hannah turned around and mounted Danny on the sofa with her panties still on. She rubbed her silk-covered pussy over his erection as he kneaded her ass with both hands under her panties, burying his face in her breasts. She clutched his head, tangling her fingers in his hair and moaning. Danny knew she was losing her inhibitions. "You're panties are soaking wet. If we keep at this my dick just might wear them thin and tear right through."

"Let's salvage them, then," she said, and stood to tear off her panties. She unbuttoned the dress all the way down and started to shrug it off, but he stopped her.

"Keep it on," he commanded. "You look hot with your clothes half-on. And then when I see you later in the office wearing that dress I can remember what you looked like when it was unbuttoned." He pulled off his pants completely, shrugging them to the floor, and unbuttoned his shirt. Hannah settled between his legs on her knees and sucked him in her expert way, deep enough so that he could feel the back of her throat with his tip. "Jesus, you're good at that," Danny groaned.

"I like to get you good and wanting me," she responded, releasing her mouth and slowly moving her body up, brushing his penis between her breasts, until she finally mounted him again with his unsheathed erection between her legs. Not yet enveloping him, she brushed her labia along his shaft. Aggressively, methodically, she dry-humped him until he was half-crazy. "How much do you want me?" she asked.

"I want you so fucking much," he cried out.

"What if I don't let you?" she asked, a fever in her eyes. "What if I just leave you like this, unfucked? What are you gonna do about it?"

Danny grabbed her shoulders like a man possessed. "I'll tear through that wet little cunt anyway and fuck you into submission." He pushed her into him so that his erect cock found its prize, bursting through her with a new intensity.

She sucked her breath in, and looked into his eyes. "I'm not submitting to you. I'm just letting you fuck me." She thrust forward with an intensity to match his. "After all, I have the high ground." She looked at him and he smiled.

He moved both hands to her shoulders and turned her away from him. "Turn around." She obeyed and spun on his member while he moved into a kneeling position on the couch. She kneeled, too, and he moved her dress out of the way and started thrusting. After a few thrusts, he grabbed her hair with one hand and pulled her up, his other hand coming over her mouth. "Who's got the high ground now?" He kept his hand over her mouth and moved the other to direct her hips. Using the skills she taught him, he thrust full and deep, stroking at just the right angle so that she could feel everything. She moaned under his hand, and he could tell that she loved him being completely in control now. He tightened his hand over her mouth, and his other hand moved to play with her clit in front of his sheathed member. He let his finger enter her a little bit. The sensation of having both inside at the same time must have been intense.

"Oh, God, Danny—I'm coming so hard my head aches!" Relentlessly, Danny kept going, and before he knew it he could feel her coming again. She was crying out under his hand, which he still hadn't removed.

"Who's in control now?" he growled as he thrust.

He moved his hand and she cried out, "You, Danny!" She fell onto her hands as she came a third time, and he finished her off with the jackhammering that he had done before with Akie, but that this time

was even more fulfilling because he knew he had more power over
Hannah than he'd ever had over Akie. He enjoyed feeling the pounding
of her flesh against him. When he came, it was victorious. He knew
that he had won, and could tell that Hannah knew it, too. Completely
spent from this latest intense romp, he knew she would do whatever he
wanted from this point forward. There was nothing that he couldn't
ask.

*

Hannah wasn't sure if things were going quite the way she had
hoped. Sure, they didn't have to drink the last time they'd gotten away
together—but they hadn't eaten, either. They hadn't done anything
except intense fucking. So it felt, even more than ever, that their
relationship was a two-sided coin: work on one side and sex on the
other. And that was it—the two sides never faced each other, and there
was certainly no room in-between for anything else. She wondered if
they could re-capture some of the carefree fun they'd shared before they
had become intimate.

Tuesday was busy with meetings, so Hannah and Danny couldn't
revisit their new rendezvous spot. Hannah wondered if maybe Wednesday she could propose a break, a trip to one of those fun new eateries in
Echo Park, or a walk around The Grove. But as soon as they drove out
of the range of the office, Danny grabbed Hannah's hand and pushed it
inside of his pants. "I need you so badly, Hannah."

It immediately broke down any resolution she had to avoid sex that
day. She felt herself start to throb despite herself, and grabbed his hand
to place it under her lacy underpants. "I need you, too." They spent the
whole drive to Silverlake pleasuring each other, so that when they got to
the rehearsal space and unlocked the door, Danny just pushed her
against the wall and pulled up her skirt. He thrust down his pants and

her underwear to the floor and said, "Now." She mounted him so that her legs were hugging around his hips and used her hand to guide him easily into her. He pressed her body against the wall and started pounding intensely. They both came within minutes.

Danny laughed. "Well, what now? Back to the office?"

Hannah was a little hurt that he'd even proposed that. "You know, we still get an hour. There's a new little eatery just about five minutes from here that I was reading about. It won't take long to catch a quick bite."

"Okay," said Danny, "As long as we can get back within an hour."

Although she was irritated at his sudden need to hurry back to the office now that he'd gotten in a quick fuck, Hannah bit her tongue. She refused to upset this opportunity to enjoy Danny's company from a completely different facet.

They found the efficient little eatery, and the food was quick and delicious. It was nice, because it gave them a chance to talk like they used to, and Hannah felt herself just a bit melancholy for the days of their close friendship. They spent so much of their time together now having sex that they really didn't get much conversation in. She had missed it.

When they got back to his car, Danny paused. "Oh, I almost forgot—" he reached to the glove compartment and got out a CD. "The first one I'm giving away. I hope you enjoy it." It was a black cover with the name "Montage" written in translucent lettering, revealing a montage of band photos underneath. Hannah could recognize the sofa from the rehearsal space.

"Really, Danny? You know I'd be willing to buy it."

Danny shook his head firmly. "You know I'd never let you do that. You have given me so much, Hannah. I don't know what I'd have done without you these past few months. You really helped keep me from feeling so alone—I guess you'll never know how much. This really is the least I can do."

Hannah held the CD to her chest. "Thank you, sweetie. I'll listen to it with pride, knowing that my magnificent friend Danny is at its heartbeat."

She realized with this gift that she still meant more to Danny than just a quick fuck—that the sex was really his way of fully expressing that. So she resolved to be worthy of this gift of his friendship, unconventional though it may be. It was selfish of her to expect anything more.

*

Danny's sex drive seemed to be on overload these days. He could barely wait until it was 11:00 Thursday before he walked over to Hannah's cubicle. She looked up, and he wordlessly nodded toward the elevator lobby. He went down to his car to wait. It's what they had taken to doing so that they didn't always leave together. The less opportunities for gossip, the better.

They had barely gotten through the door of the rehearsal space when Danny grabbed for Hannah and started kissing her greedily. He backed her into the floor, accidentally crashing into the drumset.

Hannah pushed him away, looking regrettably at the mess. "Oh, God, we've ruined it! I'm so sorry, Danny."

Danny took a moment to replace the fallen components. "It's fine—my fault. I was distracted by how hot you are."

Hannah still looked hesitant. "We should steer clear of the band's equipment."

Danny rolled his eyes. "Sit on the drumset."

Hannah looked at Danny dubiously. "Danny, I think we've already tempted fate."

He gently pushed her into the drumset. "Sit."

She smiled resignedly, obeying.

Danny grabbed one of the drumsticks, and started to unbutton his jeans. He let his erection burst forth as he pulled down his briefs. "Unbutton your blouse and unhook the front of your bra." She did so dutifully. He traced the outline of her nipple with the drumstick, then moved it down to the slit in her skirt. He tore erratically at the slit, revealing her lacy underwear. He maneuvered his cock over her crotch line, using the drumstick to pry down the top of her panties, and she helped him pull them down. He flung them aside using the drumstick. "Open your legs wide."

She opened them for him, settling her feet on the stool legs. She was completely revealed—he could see by the way her red opening flowered that she was ready to receive him already. He started to jerk repeatedly with one hand at his erection, admiring all that he saw, while he used the other to move the drumstick over the outer line of her labia. He could see her throbbing and arching in anticipation. "You trust me completely, don't you?"

She nodded. "Yes, Danny—I really do. I know you'd never willing-ly hurt me."

He flung the drumstick aside. "I trust you, too. This place is yours to use. And so am I." He pulled her away from the seat of the drumset, and led her back into the couch, where he urged her to lay down. He took her in as she lay there, looking up at him. He continued to jerk at his cock. Her beautiful face was angelic, her lips rosy and pure, and he wanted to invade them, see them wrapped around to do the devil's work. "I wanna fuck your mouth."

She opened her mouth wide, and he hovered over her so that he could face the rest of her body. He started to thrust into her mouth, and she moaned in satisfaction. She started to rub over her swelling pussy, but he pushed her hand aside. "I can take care of that." He let his fingers rub around her clit, and over her P-sponge. Only once the moans became louder did he allow one of the fingers to submerge into the darkness, making sure the rest of his hand mastered her outer parts while his finger explored the inside. She sucked instinctively harder and moaned louder, and after a few minutes he forced himself to withdraw before he could burst.

"Fuck me!" she cried out once her mouth was empty. He hastened to her other end and plunged himself into where his hand had been exploring only seconds before. Using her legs for leverage, he rhythmically dug into her, and he delved down to replace his tongue into her still-open mouth. Their kisses were once again in perfect sync, and they only stopped when he burst into her. She shrieked at the same time, body shaking, so he knew her satisfaction was complete. He settled his weight on top of her, trying hard to catch his breath. He felt drugged and perfectly content.

"Danny?" asked Hannah after a few minutes.

"Mmmhmm?"

"Wouldn't it be lovely to run away to the beach for a few hours, to make love on the sand?" She kissed the top of his head.

He felt himself drifting off. "Yeah, that'd be awesome." He yawned, enjoying the drowsy effects of her warm, perspiring body under his. "Wake me up in a few minutes, okay?"

*

It was only later, once he was driving home and began to lodge his mind back into reality, that Danny began to think about how irresponsible it was to use the band's rehearsal space for his own sexual conquests. But the truth was, he didn't know where he would take her if not there, and he just couldn't get enough of Hannah's body. She wasn't the most classically beautiful or voluptuous woman, but something about her was so intoxicating and addictive. He never knew sex with the same woman, over and over, could be so intense. He only needed to think about her pink lips and her pink pussy, and he'd go hard all over again.

There was no doubt, Hannah was amazing. But complicated—too complicated. She was still healing from the divorce (even if she didn't choose to admit it to herself), and her life with two half-custody children was not one he was ready to join. Even if he was, he still wanted a life in the music industry. That meant being able to travel across the country for a gig at a moment's notice. A woman responsible for the well-being of two kids couldn't do that, and he knew Hannah was so attached and supportive that she'd try. And then her family would suffer in the aftermath. No, Hannah just didn't fit into Danny's plans for success, not in the long run.

That still didn't mean they couldn't have fun while it lasted. It was another three-day weekend, and that was a long time to wait for Hannah again. Maybe she would be open to the idea of meeting tomorrow— after all, her kids were still in school on Fridays, even though she had every other one off. He'd never thought to ask her if she wanted to hang out on a Friday, and wasn't sure if she'd be game, but it certainly couldn't hurt to try. As he walked into his apartment, he started to text her to ask. But his message was still mid-composition when an incoming call came in. He couldn't believe the image he saw on the screen. Akie.

"Akie?"

"Hey, Danny—long time, no talk." Her voice sounded hesitant.

"I just didn't want to bother Miss Busy Music Exec," he said playfully. "How's Tokyo?"

"Danny, I'm back in L.A."

He paused—shit, he'd been so preoccupied with Hannah that he'd lost track. "Weren't you looking at June?"

"Yeah, I finished up early and was just sorta tired of Tokyo. Look, I know this is asking a lot, but my place is still sublet until June and I need a place to stay." Danny's head was spinning—he couldn't believe the track had changed this fast. "Danny, are you still there?"

"Yeah, uh, yes—of course, Akie, you can stay with me. I got plenty of room. Where are you right now?"

"Tom Bradley International Terminal."

"Okay, I'll be right there to pick you up. Should only take me, like, 30 minutes. Sit tight, and I'll text you when I'm outside of the terminal." Shit. This was really unexpected. How was he supposed to deal with having Akie back, when he'd just been ready to text Hannah and ask her to hang out tomorrow? He hastily went back to his messages and erased what he'd written so far. Anyway, he couldn't assume anything where Akie was concerned. After all, they'd parted friends. He had no right to think that anything would happen, just because he was letting her crash at his place for a month. But then wasn't that the whole goal of this thing with Hannah in the first place? To win back Akie?

The 405 Freeway had a way of bringing a mind back to the present moment, and for the next half hour he just focused on trying to get to the terminal. Once there, he texted Akie and waited to see her voluptuous outline. She didn't disappoint. She was in some skinny jeans and a tank top, and her breasts peeked enticingly out of the scooped neck. Thick, strappy sandals added height to her already tall frame, and she pulled a large suitcase with an attaché behind her. He jumped out of the car.

"Here, let me help you with that, Akie." He grabbed the suitcase handle from her, and leaned over to embrace her.

"Danny, thank you so much for coming to get me on such short notice!"

"What was I gonna do, strand you at the airport?" He rolled the bags over to the back of his SUV, and popped the trunk. After putting them in the back, he opened the passenger door for Akie. He was glad it had been over a week since he and Hannah had messed around in there.

Once he settled into the driver's seat and put the car into gear, he started talking. "So you couldn't stay with your mom?"

He could see Akie shrug out of the corner of his eye. "I guess I could've, but then I'd have to deal with her asking me about Tokyo and the guy I was dating there, and why it didn't work out. I just didn't feel like dealing with that tonight. Too tired."

"I get it," said Danny. "So why didn't it work out?"

Akie smacked his arm. "None of your business!"

He laughed. "I'm just saying, the more you tell, the better your lodging."

"That's so mean!"

"That's strategy," he said matter-of-factly.

"Let's just say—even though my mom would've been delighted at the match—he wasn't the guy for me." She leaned her head against the passenger seat and he could feel her gaze on him. "He was missing— something."

"Fair enough," said Danny. They spent the next half hour talking about Akie's adventures in Tokyo, about the music scene there, and he realized just how much he missed that life that he'd had. Sure, fire and police stations had kept him eating for the past year, but music was his passion. It reminded him that his current job was something for which he had settled, and it was time to stop being complacent and jump-start his career.

When they got back to his place, Danny turned on the sound system. "Hey, I want you to hear the new EP we put together." He set it to play, and he noticed that Akie really was listening intently. "You relax—I'll whip something up for us to eat."

He had some pre-cooked chicken in the fridge and threw together a salad with the produce he got from his weekly Farmers Market box, then popped a bottle of white wine he'd been saving for a special occasion. He poured two glasses, and brought them over to the sofa, where the EP had just finished the last song. Akie looked up. "It's really good, Danny. Very cutting edge. Do you mind if I bring it to my boss?"

"You can bring it to anyone in the music industry you want. Thanks."

"Hey, it's still my job to keep Unchained current, and Montage certainly is that. Thank you." She took a sip of the wine. "That's good, too."

"Just a taste of the fine things you'll be eating tonight. Hungry?"

"You made dinner that fast? Wow, you really are spoiling me."

Danny smiled. "Don't get too excited. It's just a salad with some pre-cooked chicken."

"Danny, I'm so hungry it sounds like a feast—let's eat!"

He took her hand and led her over to the table, where the salad was already plated. He'd made sure that the produce was presented nicely. "I never get a chance to use all this produce they send me every week, so you're really doing me a favor by helping me eat it."

Akie smiled as she sat down. "Oh, Danny—I am so happy to be back in good ol' SoCal. Look at these veggies! What a great meal to have my first night back!" She looked up at him, eyebrow raised suggestively. "I'm happy to do you more favors, if you want."

"One favor at a time," said Danny, and he sat down beside her.

They enjoyed the salad, and polished off the wine, too. Conversation flowed freely, as Danny told her all about his challenges with trying to market public places that may or may not be welcome in the neighborhood. She seemed interested in what he told her, and asked lots of questions about the work, and about the people he worked with. Danny even told her about Hannah—but he was careful not to tell Akie about how close they had become. He mentioned her only as part of a group that he'd shared some fun times with.

Akie sat back in her seat. "Well, Danny—I'm glad you've been able to re-establish yourself so well. I know it's not what you want to do, but it seems like you do it well, and you have some good people to work with. That's sometimes more important than the thing you do." She stretched her arms out, yawning. "There's nothing I'd love so much as a hot shower—you think you could make that happen for me?"

"It could be arranged. You know, I was thinking of just camping out in the room I use as a studio. I have a daybed pushed against the wall in there. You can make yourself at home in the master bedroom— I'll just get you some fresh towels. Come on." He led her to the back of his apartment. "I'll leave you to it. Oh, and I'll grab your suitcase out of the car while you get cleaned up. I'll leave it by the door in the hallway."

"Thanks, Danny." Akie reached up and kissed him long on the lips. He looked down at her for a moment after, and then turned to go get her bag.

He waited until he heard the shower going, and then went out to the car to get her suitcase. As he was laying it by the outside of the door to the master bedroom, he heard her calling. "Danny?" He opened the door and went into the bedroom. She was still in the shower, so he popped his head into the steamy room.

"I'm here."

"There's no shampoo."

"Oh, it's in the cabinet under the sink." He moved to leave, but her voice stopped him.

"Could you get it for me, Danny? There's no bath rug, and I don't want to slip on the tiles."

"Sure," he said, and he fetched the desired bottle. "Do you want me to pass it over the door?"

She slid it open, wet body shining in the bright lights of his bath-room. "You can just give it to me." He looked longingly at her jet-black hair, which stuck to her glistening breasts, her fully waxed pubis, and her curvy hips, speechless. She smiled. "Why don't you join me?"

"I'm, um, kinda fully dressed."

She flicked water in his face. "Well, then get un-fully dressed!"

For a split second, Danny thought of saying no—it seemed a little indulgent to have Akie the same day he'd had Hannah. But then the next split second told him he'd be crazy to say no to the woman he'd wanted for so long, the one he'd schemed to get with Hannah's crazy tutelage. Here was his chance to put all he'd learned into action. Eagerly, he undid his shirt and whipped off his shoes and pants. Free from his clothes, he stepped into the shower behind Akie. "I have to say," he said as he kissed the back of her neck, "I didn't expect to be doing *this* tonight." He reached around and fondled her luscious breasts gently with one hand, tickling her nipples between his thumb and index finger, and then moved his other hand to caress her water-lodged pussy. He made sure to hit all the spots from the outside, knowing that she probably wasn't ready for anything to enter just yet.

Akie thrust her head back into his chest. "Oh, Danny—that feels so good!"

"I agree," he said. He moved to face her, so that the water from the shower was hitting him from behind. "I may need a little help getting ready," he said, pushing her hand to his half-erect cock. He wasn't sure why it wasn't completely ready to go—probably because he'd sort of tired it out with Hannah earlier.

Akie locked her hand around it and jerked it gently. "It's kind of difficult to go down in the shower, you know."

"Well, then let's get out of the shower," he said, turning off the shower head. He got out first, grabbing the towel off the rack so that he could dry her off a little before she emerged. After all this, it *would* suck for her to slip on the tile floor. "Just like a car wash," he said as he dripped on the floor, "Except your body is much better than any car's." He laid the towel on the floor, and held her hand as she stepped out.

She laughed. "What service," was all she was able to utter before he caught her mouth in a kiss. It wasn't as well-timed as those he'd shared with Hannah, but it was still arousing. Akie broke away. "Could you do that a little further down?"

"My pleasure," he said, and he sunk down to his knees to give her oral pleasure. It was fun to do that again—after all, it had been one of his best natural talents. Akie moaned. The sound turned him on, and he reached down to jerk at himself to strengthen his erection. He was able to get it pretty hard.

"Danny, let's go into the bedroom." He looked up, and she reached for his hand. She led him into the bedroom, where she laid her still-wet head on the bed.

"I still gotta dry off a little before I lay down," he said. "Get on your hands and knees." Eyebrows raised, she got in the desired position, and Danny pulled her toward him by her hips. He placed his cock between her legs, and held it against her clit with one hand, while the other guided her hips in a back-and-forth motion. Seeming to catch on quickly, Akie took over holding his cock in place, while he reached to continue fondling her breasts. He moved the other hand to the base of her back.

"Oh, man—Danny, that's really amazing!"

"I'm here to please you," he said. He continued to tantalize her, until he felt her get wetter on his hard on. "It feels like you're just about ready."

"Yes, Danny—please!"

He distracted her for a moment while he reached into the bedside table to grab a condom. "You sure you want it?"

"I want it!"

"What do you want?" he asked as he slipped the latex over his erection.

"I want you to fuck me!"

He maneuvered to the back of her, allowing her to push him into her slick canal, and he bent his knees to stroke her full and hard. She cried out involuntarily. He slowed down, still keeping the pressure hard, but making sure to play with the friction that he was causing. "You need to be taught a lesson, young lady. You went away without giving me another chance to put that little cunt in its place."

"Yes, Danny, teach me a lesson!"

He grabbed her still wet hair, and she was upright against him. He grabbed between her thighs with one hand, and cupped his arm around her breasts, allowing his hand to rub against one. "This is one they can't teach you in Tokyo." He dug into her deep, pushing her bottom against him. He then allowed his finger to play with her clit while he thrust.

"Oh, fuck, Danny!" He felt her body tense, and he knew she was coming hard.

"Oh, we're not done yet," he said, and he continued to stroke her fully and aggressively. Her body soon tensed again, and she shrieked like he'd never heard. He figured he'd demonstrated what he could do, and allowed himself to go full force into her. He didn't come as hard as he had earlier, but he figured that was because he was a little tired. They collapsed together, still wet on the bed.

"Holy shit," said Akie, "Third time's a charm. Being away from you has made all the difference in the world."

Danny just smiled sleepily beside her. He knew it was more than that—he knew it was Hannah's training. But he would let that remain a secret.

He woke the next morning from the sunlight streaming into the master bedroom. Akie was sitting up next to him. She turned when she saw he'd awaken. "I'm glad you're awake, Danny. I've been thinking."

He stretched his eyes open and tried to focus on her. "I hope that's a good thing."

"You tell me, Danny. Look, I know we parted on sorta whatever terms last year. You had offered to share your life with me, and I—well, I guess I just wasn't ready for that. I think it took almost a year in a foreign country to realize where I need to be."

Danny sat up in the bed, too. "And where is that?"

"Here. With you. Danny, is that offer of marriage still on the table?"

Danny hesitated—he couldn't be dreaming, could he? But her beautiful face was there before him, looking at him as if what he said could make or break the rest of her life. "Of course it is, Akie."

"Then let's run off to Vegas. Tonight."

"What—Akie—don't you want your mother there, your family? Don't you want a wedding with flowers and a harp player and shit?"

"No, Danny—I don't want any of that shit. What do you say?"

Danny felt totally railroaded. But then he checked himself. This was his chance for a healthy relationship, one that he could mutually build with a woman who had no strings attached—except maybe a disapproving family, but whatever. Sure, the sex may not be as porn star as what he'd been used to lately. But this was life, not SkineMax.

"Let's do it," he said.

Track 7

Why did anyone ever schedule important meetings on Mondays? That's the thought that kept driving through Hannah's brain as she tried to finish putting together a marketing presentation that she and Danny had started for the fire station. They'd spent a lot of time fucking around last week, so hadn't really gotten everything as ready as she normally liked things to be for a presentation that would be first thing after a long weekend. She wondered disappointedly if she and Danny would be able to get away for lunch again. It seemed like today promised to be pretty jam-packed with work.

She had so much she wanted to talk about with him, too—if he'd give her a chance to talk. She'd listened to the EP, and even though it was good she felt it was missing something—a certain degree of raw honesty, maybe? That honesty that comes from peeling your heart open and putting it on display. It had been in Danny's Exquisite Corpse work. She wondered if the collaboration was at the loss of what made Danny's music uniquely Danny. He wasn't a native Angelino, but his music had a sound that was unfiltered and completely Los Angeles—and then his life near the ocean could be heard in some of the musical interludes—sort of a blend of amplified chaos meets deep, expansive reflection.

It must be lovely at the beach today.

Unexpectedly, Eduardo knocked on the opening of her cubicle. "Hannah, we have a major change of plans."

"What's wrong?"

He put up his hands. "Nothing wrong really, but your partner in crime decided to take a few days off."

"What? Is he okay?"

Eduardo snorted. "Oh, yeah, he's okay. Really okay. It appears he got married over the weekend!"

Hannah felt like he'd just thrown a bowling ball at her gut, and all she could do was try to stand. "Wh-what? Danny got married—how?"

"I think they did a Vegas thing. Anyway, don't feel left out. Sounds like no one was invited. They're still over there, so I need you to make the presentation to the GM. You think you can make it work without Danny?"

She channeled all the acting lessons she'd ever had as a teen and forced the biggest smile that she could muster. "It'll be better without him."

Eduardo's guffaw was uncertain and boisterous. "There's the spirit! Okay, I'll see you in an hour." And off he walked, not having a clue that he'd just ripped her world apart with the information he'd disclosed.

Danny—married? How? Why would he choose to be so hasty— and to allow her to find out this way? Didn't he owe her at the very least the chance to be told by him personally? They just had sex last week—repeatedly! Did it really mean so little to him? Heartbroken, she realized that *this* indicated exactly that.

Hannah could have never thought it possible to make an important, professional presentation while her heart was in the process of breaking, especially on a topic with which she was only partially familiar. Her job as the project manager was to coordinate the finance and contract pieces, make sure construction was on track, and to get all the Council Authority in order. She hadn't been focused exclusively on the market-ing piece, and so really had to reach back into her schooling to present what had been prepared. Her heart was so numb that she had no way of assessing how she'd done, but Eduardo approached her afterwards and told her he was so impressed that he wanted her to do another for the Neighborhood Council in a few days. She supposed in any other circumstances she would have been motivated and proud—but now she was just sad, so incredibly sad.

*

"Here comes the married man!" Hannah could hear Dominic's loud voice, and she just wanted to tell him to shut up. Not only was it heartbreaking to hear all this joy over what she perceived to be a betrayal—it was humiliating. She simply focused on the PowerPoint that she was creating, and tried to ignore the tears that stung at her eyes. With any luck, Danny would just stay away from her now that he didn't have a use for her.

No such luck. He knocked on the outside of her cubicle a half hour later. "Hey, Hannah."

She kept her eyes focused on her computer screen. "Hey, yourself."

"Guess you've heard my news, huh?"

"Who hasn't—it's all anybody talks about."

Danny chuckled. "Yeah, I guess I'm the last guy they've thought would take the plunge, huh? But I'll bet you knew it was bound to happen all along, huh?"

Hannah couldn't belief how pissed and how hurt she was, all at the same time. "I'm really busy right now. Some of us had to take up the reins while you were in Vegas."

"Aw, man—thank you for that, Hannah. I guess I kinda left you high and dry there, didn't I?"

Hannah turned from her computer to cast a piercing glare into his eyes. "I guess you did."

"Thanks for being a good sport about it, though."

"Danny, is this conversation going anywhere? Because if it's not, I have work to do."

"Can I take you to lunch at least?"

"I don't have time." She turned back to her computer.

"It can be a working lunch—I should be helping you with that presentation, anyway."

"I don't need your help, Danny."

"Sure you do. Come on, Hannah—we're both professionals. We're gonna need to learn to work together."

She lost it. "Don't talk to me about working together, Danny! Where were you on Monday? Where were you the whole weekend, for that matter? You certainly weren't with me! I swung it here just fine without you, so don't do me any favors now!"

Eduardo popped his head in her cubicle. "Hannah, you getting Danny up to speed on where we are with those marketing presentations?" He looked at her admonishingly.

Danny turned to Eduardo. "Totally—she's just giving me a hard time, right Hannah? You know how we are—Hannah's always gotta get a dig in just to make sure I know who's boss." He winked at Hannah, and she seriously wanted to punch him. "We were just talking about doing an extended lunch meeting to put all the final wheels in motion."

Eduardo looked appeased. "Great! By the way, Danny—congratulations. I'll bet you ran to it before she could change her mind, huh?"

Danny smiled sheepishly. "Something like that."

"Alright, you two, I'll see you later. Have a productive lunch, okay?" The last he said while walking away down the hall.

Hannah turned back to her computer, and Danny paused. "Well—I'll see you in the lobby at Noon, okay?" Hannah didn't respond. She'd rather die a thousand painful deaths than condescend to meet with Danny for lunch. She realized she hadn't been showing a lot of self-respect lately, but no time like the present to start practicing good habits.

Noon rolled around, and Hannah continued her work. Eduardo stopped by her desk on the way back from someone else's. "Hannah, I thought you had a lunch meeting with Danny."

Hannah turned to face her boss. "According to him I did, but—Eduardo, I really need to put my time into working on this Power-Point."

Eduardo raised his eyebrows. "Hannah, I need you to get Danny up to speed. We can't stumble on this thing, okay? I'd rather the Power-Point be imperfect and have my two top players on their game. I know you did really well on the last presentation, but now that Danny's back I want you to work on this one together, okay?"

Hannah sighed. "Alright, Eduardo. I want this to be a success as much as you do, you know that, right?"

Eduardo's look softened. "I know. Now come on—make my A-Team shine!"

Hannah forced a smile, then wearily tromped to the elevator lobby. She took it down to the ground floor, where Danny was waiting. "There you are! What do you feel like today?"

"I feel like eating at my desk. But Eduardo wants this to happen, so it's happening."

Danny touched her shoulder, and she pushed his hand away. "Hannah, come on. Let's continue this conversation in the car, okay? You're really respected around here, and I don't want to see you compromise your professionalism."

Hannah was livid. "Wow—you're really one to talk about professionalism, aren't you, Danny?"

Hastily, Danny grabbed her back with one hand and shoulder with the other, and steered her toward the door to the parking lot. "Come on, let's go." She tried to shake him off, but his hands remained firmly in place until he'd prodded her into his car. When he got in, he started talking again. "Look, I didn't realize Akie would be back so soon. I really wasn't ready for what you and I had to just *end*."

"Aw, really, Danny? Gosh, that is so fucking sweet of you. I'm just so glad I could amuse you while you waited for your Aphrodite to finally decide to give you the time of day. You're a real example of how true love wins out in the end."

"Hannah, come on—that isn't fair."

"I know, I know—I'm getting all *sensitive* on you when I really should have known better. I really have to apologize, Danny, but I was under the strange impression that I *meant* something to you. That was stupid of me—I guess I need to be grateful that you would have ever condescended to fuck a real dog like me."

"Hannah, this is not about your looks or any of that—you know I still think you're one of the hottest women I've ever seen up close."

Hannah laughed hysterically. "Oh, wow—thanks, Danny. I'm feeling so special now."

"Hannah, come on—just give me a shot to explain this."

"Explain how you fucked me one day and married her the next?"

"It's not what I meant to happen. Look, when you proposed what you did you said it was so I could guarantee that the next time I saw Akie she'd never want to leave me again. And you were right—it *worked!*"

"Gosh, Danny, and I feel so fucking proud—I'm the proudest whore in Los Angeles!"

Danny reached over and grabbed her shoulders. "Hannah, stop! I'm not gonna sit here and listen to you talk about yourself like that. You're my friend and I want you to know that I have nothing but respect for you."

"Well, as long as *you* respect me…"

"Stop being so sarcastic! You know I do. You're beautiful and sensitive and so fucking smart. I've never met anyone like you. You're really one of the best friends I've ever had—you made me see things in myself that I didn't want to see, and I'm better because of that."

"I'm glad you're better. Kinda sucks to be me right now."

"Look, we talked about this months ago. This was just a fun little side note to our relationship, nothing serious. I thought we were on the exact same page."

"I'm glad you had your fun."

"Hannah, it became more than that for me. You *know* it did! I'm really glad we became so close. But you have your life and I've got mine, and they just *don't* mesh together outside of our time here at work. And what I've got with Akie—well, we just *fit* together better. She's got her job in the music business, I'm in an up-and-coming band…"

Hannah couldn't believe her ears. "So this is all about what's best for your chances in the music business? This is about who gives you a bigger boost towards a better lunch ticket?"

"No, Hannah, that's not what I meant. It's just we're in the same business and we understand each other. I forgot a little bit about the bigger picture of my life and my career. Until I saw her again. It made me realize: I was just trying to get back afloat, and then I just became complacent with this City gig. I gotta stop letting my life be about settling!"

"So being with me was settling? And now that you have Akie you don't need to settle for second best anymore?"

"No, Hannah, that's not what I meant—"

"You know what? *Fuck* you, Danny. I honestly don't give a shit if Eduardo gets pissed. I wouldn't eat with you again to save my soul." She stormed out of the car and refused to look back.

*

Danny couldn't get it together the rest of the week, or the week after. His argument with Hannah had shaken him to the core. He hadn't
expected her to be that mad. Hurt, maybe, but not so utterly pissed that
he couldn't even get across just how hard it was for him to walk away
from what they had, for both their good. He didn't know how to
explain that what she needed was someone that was much more solid
than he could ever be, and that he needed to be in a world that was
completely flexible and without walls. In saving her from him, he'd
seemed to hurt her even more. And now he'd lost one of the only
people he'd ever connected with on a truly spiritual level. Because that
really was what even the sex had been with Hannah. It was like becoming connected to something so much more powerful and all-knowing
than each of them individually. When he'd been with Hannah, he felt
completely aware of every possibility that existed in that moment. He
never worried about the past or the future. Time suspended for them,
and it was a place ripe with opportunity and elevated awareness. He
could almost see to the better person he could become when he was
inside of her.

Sex with his new wife was good, too—but it sure didn't have the
intensity of Hannah. It was much more comfortable since that first
night—he'd tried to join her in the shower a few times, but Akie would
just tell him she wanted to get clean. When they did fuck he could tell
she loved it—but she never did try to please him the way Hannah had.
It hadn't bothered him until he went to work one day and seen Hannah
in the hall, wearing that red shirtdress she'd worn when she'd blown him
on the sofa in the rehearsal space and then tortured him with her
soaking wet pussy. He got a near-erection just seeing her, and then
when he'd passed by she'd walked the other way, refusing to even
acknowledge him. He found himself jacking off in the shower that
night, instead of climbing into bed with his wife.

Danny wondered if it was time to move on from this job.

It was a Saturday in mid-June when he and Akie were eating brunch at a place in Santa Monica, and she mentioned Montage's EP.

"So I've been thinking it'd be great to promote your band through Unchained. I hope you don't mind, but I set up a meeting this week with all the big mucky-mucks over there. They heard the EP and they want to hear more."

"Akie, that's awesome! Thank you so much! You give me the time and the place, and I'll get the guys over there."

Danny took the Thursday of the meeting off from work to get the band ready. They had to establish what their minimum terms would be, so that they could come into the meeting as a unified front. Danny knew this business, and he knew that even with Akie as his wife Montage could get seriously taken advantage of unless they showed that they knew their worth.

They walked into Unchained's office with the uncompromising air of the next big thing in music—and they walked out with an offer over three times better than their agreed-upon minimum. They celebrated with afternoon drinks at the Rainbow Room. Danny hadn't drank that much since his pre-Akie days, and he woke the next morning with a brutal hangover and passionate resolve to quit his job with the City. It was clearly a safe move, now that he had practically signed the contract. As he drove down the 10 toward Downtown that morning, he realized he really wouldn't miss too much about working there. Except Hannah. But she wasn't really talking to him anymore anyway. He wished he knew a way to salvage their friendship.

He put in his two-week notice that Friday.

The next two weeks were non-stop, with Danny trying to get everything in as much order as possible for when they hired the next marketing guy. He communicated a lot with Hannah about the fire station over e-mail, since she really wouldn't allow him to talk to her for any length of time. She always acted like she had somewhere else she needed to be. But he could see that her eyelids were puffy. He felt like such an asshole.

They didn't speak at length until he was walking towards Eduardo's office on his last day, for an end-of-the-day briefing on where he was at with every assignment. As usual, Hannah was on the run to catch her train. As she whizzed by, he lightly touched her arm. "Hannah."

She stopped, looking around awkwardly. "So is this goodbye?" He could see tears springing to her eyes.

"Only for now. I'm always nearby, if you ever needs a friend." He smiled, and started to lean toward her.

"I need a friend, but not one like you." It stopped Danny, and he straightened out. "But I'm glad things are working out for you."

"Not in every department, it appears," said Danny. "I miss you."

Hannah lost control of the tears, and they poured over her sweet cheekbones. "Don't make this harder for me than it already is, Danny. Let's just part ways and wish each other luck, okay?" She offered her hand for him to shake. Danny impulsively grabbed it and started to pull her toward him in an embrace, but Hannah jerked away. "I'm sorry, I can't. Goodbye, Danny." She turned brusquely and hurried toward the elevator.

Danny felt his heart sink at the thought of never seeing her again. *Push it to the back of your mind,* he told himself. He supposed some things you just bury in a safe place, where no one can get a hold of them. Hannah was exactly that sort of treasure.

*

The contract was near-inked by July. Danny was waiting in a conference room at Unchained with Gavin, Mark, and their drummer Chem, while the lawyers worked out some final details of their contract. He couldn't believe it was finally happening.

"Hey, Gav—can you believe where we are?"

Gavin smiled. "Yeah, happy birthday, man. Who'd'of thunk when we had this crazy idea two years ago that we'd be signing a contract with one of the biggest indie labels in the industry? I know it has a lot to do with Akie, Danny—so thank you. She really came through for us…Which reminds me…" Gavin looked at Mark and then Chem, who both nodded at him as if he should continue. "So, look, Danny, Chem noticed a few weeks ago before you got to practice that someone'd been fucking with his drumset—it was all messed up from what it had been just two days ago. We were really worried that someone was getting into the rehearsal space, so we asked security to dig into their tapes from the day before."

Danny put his head down. "Oh, man, why didn't you tell me?"

"We were gonna, but then you were kinda late so we just needed to get on the ball. Anyway, a few days ago the security guy called me and said he had a video of someone going into the rehearsal space during the day that we didn't have practice. I went over there, and he replayed it for me. Imagine my surprise when I saw an overhead of you and your little blond M.I.L.F."

"Aw, man—Gav, I'm sorry."

"Look, Danny, what you do with your cock is none of my business, until it has the power to affect this deal we have. Then it's all my business. Your little lunchtime romps with Hannah have to stop."

Danny nodded. "Already handled, Gav. I was going a little wild before I became an old married man, but Hannah and I are through."

"So you're not gonna fuck this up for us?"

"No way, man. Look, I was in a bind and she was really ready—and I just sorta thought with my dick. But it won't happen again."

"So you're done."

"Totally done. For now." Danny winked.

"You *fucking* DICK!" It was Akie. He hadn't noticed the door was ajar, and she'd been listening the whole time. She stormed out of the office.

"Shit," said Danny, running his fingers through his hair.

"What the fuck, man? You better go get her and make this shit right!" Gavin was looking at him like he wanted to punch him.

"Alright, alright," said Danny, running out to follow her. She was fumbling with the key to his car when he approached.

"Akie—wait! I'm sorry."

She looked over at him with an icy glare and opened the driver's side. Danny hurried into the passenger seat. She turned the car toward the Westside. "What the *fuck* Danny? Who were you sleeping with while I was in Japan? Was it that little cunt you keep talking about from your old office?"

He couldn't believe how pissed he felt hearing Akie say bad things about Hannah. "There's no need for name calling, and that's beside the point. I didn't even know if you were coming back, or if you would ever let us be more than friends!"

Akie stared straight at the road. "Were you messing around with her when you were calling me and begging me to come back to the States?"

Danny groaned. "It didn't roll out like that. Come on, Akie—you were with what's his name in Tokyo, and you don't hear me getting all butt-hurt because of it."

"Butt-hurt? Butt-hurt?"

"You know what I mean. We weren't committed in any way, not until the night you got back. I had no expectations."

"Fucking-A...When did it stop?"

Danny paused. "I never messed around once we were married."

Akie looked like she'd blow her top. "Goddammit, *when did it stop, Danny?*"

He took a deep breath. "The day you got back."

Akie, pulled the car over without warning, a barrage of blaring horns following. "The same day we had sex, you had already fucked another woman?"

"Yes."

"Get out of the fucking car, Danny!"

Danny stayed in his seat. "What do you mean get out of the car? This is my car."

"Fine." Akie swung the driver's side door open and strutted angrily to the sidewalk.

"Akie, where are you going?!" he shouted after her.

"The *fuck* away from you!"

He didn't know why, but he made no move to go after or to stop her. As she barged away, all Danny could think was that he was relieved that everything was out in the open, and that there was nothing left to hide. He figured she'd just blow off some steam and then come home to figure things out.

But when he got home, he waited. Akie never showed. He tried calling her cell, but it just went to voicemail. He texted her. "FUCK OFF!" was the answer she provided.

A phone call at 9:00 the next morning woke Danny. He had fallen asleep on the sofa. Hazy, he answered it. "Hello?"

"Danny, where did you go yesterday? The contract was about to be inked and you didn't come back!" It was Gavin.

"Dude, you *told* me to go after her!"

"Go after and come back! But you didn't come back, and when they got to the conference room with the final contract we weren't all able to sign. I told them I'd get you back first thing, then I get a call at fucking 8:00 in the morning that I need to get the fuck over there. She's fixing it so that they won't make the deal as long as you're in the band."

Danny was shocked that Akie would be this relentless in her wrath. "Did you tell them to fuck off?"

"No, man—I couldn't."

"What the—"

Gavin sounded just as angry. "Look, Danny, this is the chance of a lifetime. And if we don't get a new bass player, we lose it."

Danny couldn't believe his ears. "Gav—you're my best friend."

"I know, man—but I have a family now, and they have to come first. I'm sorry, man. You're out." The phone was hung up. Danny just sat there, motionless.

Out. Out of the band, out of a job, out of a wife. Happy fucking birthday.

*

Later that week, Gavin called Danny, and they did their best to mend fences. Danny tried to understand Gavin's point of view, and they hung up on okay terms. But he felt so betrayed that his friend would choose to cut him to save face with the record label. It was infuriating—but he couldn't really stand on any high ground here. What Gavin had done to Danny was pretty much exactly what Danny had done to Hannah.

Hannah.

Over the next few weeks, Danny found himself realizing, hard as all these losses had been, it wasn't the band he was missing, and certainly not Akie. The bitch had blackballed him in the music marketing industry, as well as stolen his dream of success in a band, and he honestly wasn't sure what he was going to do to make money now.

The one thing he missed above all else, now that he had nothing, was Hannah.

She was the one true thing that he had, and he let her go because of what he thought he wanted with Akie. But Hannah was really everything he ever needed. Somewhere deep down he had known it, known it when the world stopped every time they were together. But he'd been afraid to lose himself to the obligations he thought would be imposed by a commitment to Hannah. So Akie was the easy way out. The cheap, easy way out, and the fast track to stardom.

What an idiot.

He'd masterfully avoided everything that was true in his life, from Hannah, who made him feel more than he ever thought was possible, to his music. And now she was gone.

All Danny could think about was Hannah, and he thought he was going crazy. Until the thought triggered a flood of memories, and the memories gave way to a song. It was a song that had been buried in his consciousness all along, the one he heard when he was with her. And he had to write it down.

He didn't want to forget a love that was that real.

Finale: 10 Months Later

Hannah woke to the faint smell of lavender in the air. It was so nice to be able to use the open windows to keep the house cool at night—South Pasadena was so much cooler during the spring than where she had been living. And lavender could actually sustain in the garden.

Her 10-year-old ran into the bedroom. "Time to get up, mom!"

"Ugh, *man*—how did you get into my side?"

He laughed. "Daddy says that's the advantage to duplex living!"

"Daddy is mean. Okay, fine—give me like a half-hour to get ready, okay? I know your dad still has to feed you." She was so glad to be able to see the kids on the weekdays again. She hadn't regretted once that she and her ex had decided to move into this cute little duplex, sharing the mortgage. It was closer to the City, and they had gotten into a good rhythm with the kids.

Work was something worth getting up for. When Danny left, she'd had to take up his marketing duties, and had been better at it than she thought she would be. She was given more responsibilities, and eventually Eduardo was able to use the money that was saved on Danny's salary to create a new position for her. She was making more money, and doing what she'd always dreamed. Tired as hell, but it was a good, fulfilling tired.

When she'd heard all that had happened to Danny, she was so sad for him, but hesitated in reaching out. She knew that she needed to get her life together before she could try to fix anyone else's. And he had hurt her so much. When she had finally mustered the courage to contact him, her texts and e-mails came back as undelivered. She often thought with a smile about all the joy he'd given her, and prayed that he was somehow okay.

There was never much time to sit and ponder the past, though. Her schedule required her to get the kids to daycare with plenty of time for the daycare folks to cart them over to their school. She had it down to a science.

The morning was the same as others: drop off the kids, catch the Gold Line, then hop on the Red Line. She didn't think much when she saw a bunch of rose petals scattered on the street-level entrance to the Civic Center Station as she came up the escalator. She had to blink for a minute when she saw a completely-uniformed driver holding up a placard with her name on it: HANNAH MERCURY. Bewildered, Hannah approached the driver.

"Ms. Mercury?" he asked.

Hannah was totally confused now. "That's me."

The driver waved to an old-fashioned Cadillac, illegally parked in the bus stop. "Please, ma'am."

Hannah looked at the driver suspiciously. "I'm sorry, but I don't know you and wasn't told by my boss that there would be any—"

She was interrupted by the buzzing of her phone. She looked down at the display, but the number was unrecognizable. "Hello?"

"Come on, you know you're curious." She knew him the second he spoke.

All of a sudden, the old hurt started to rise back up. Tears forming, she said in a semi-steady voice, "I was curious that first happy hour, and look where it got me."

"I know, Hannah—and I am begging you to please just give me a chance."

Hannah looked at the Cadillac, and wondered if she would ever be able to forgive herself if she didn't listen to that calmly growing murmur in her heart, telling her to trust love. She decided to get in.

The car drove them to the 110 freeway going south, and then cut over to the 10 West. It didn't stop until it hit the beach, and then kept traveling the long road up the coast. It was a stunning day in May, and Hannah realized that it had been exactly a year since she and Danny had last made love.

After what seemed like the longest drive she'd ever had to endure, the car stopped on a small road, fronting a secluded beach. The door was opened for her, and the driver helped her out of the car.

Danny was there, holding a yellow rose.

Hannah approached him deliberately. "The beach, huh? I thought you forgot."

"I only acted like I did." He handed her the rose.

She bent her face down to breathe in its sweet fragrance. "For friendship, huh?" He looked confused. "The yellow rose—it means friendship."

Danny looked rather annoyed at himself. "Is that what it means? Oh. I got it because it's yellow, like the sun. Like you." Hannah tilted her blond head inquisitively. "I mean, my life—you light it up."

Hannah laughed. "Maybe it's good you stopped writing lyrics." Their eyes locked. "I'm sorry, Danny—that was harsh. I heard what happened with the band. You deserved more."

Danny gave her a smile that she'd never seen, one that betrayed a whole lot of hardship that he hadn't seen before. "Thanks, Hannah. Turns out I got exactly what I deserved. And it's exactly what *needed* to happen to light a fire under my ass." He reached for something off a stand, and Hannah realized it was a guitar. "This is for you, too."

Hannah put her hand up. "Danny, before you do anything, please know this doesn't change anything. You really hurt me—you saw me hurting about Connor and then you went and did the exact same thing that he did—what you did was worse!"

"Hannah, please. If this is it, just let me live out this one last fantasy. Let me sing my song to my girl—even if she's only mine for the three minutes it takes to sing it."

"Your girl?" She couldn't believe how amazing the idea sounded, but she shook it off, trying to look nonchalant. "You wrote a new song?"

"I wrote a new album. This is the best song on it. It's about us."

Hannah crossed her arms. "I thought you didn't like telling people who or what your songs are about."

"You're not people. You're Hannah. And this is your song." He started to strum his guitar in a slow, melancholy tune:

I WANDERED ON THE OCEAN,
SELFISH AND ALONE.
AND CAME UPON A PARADISE,
PERFECT AND UNKNOWN.

AND ON THAT PERFECT BEACH,
WHERE THE SEAGULLS FLEW AND PLAYED
I FOUND A HIDDEN TREASURE,
IN THE CREEPING TIDE SHE LAID.

PARADISE, I LOST YOU
I'M CRYING OUT TO PARADISE ALONE.

REVEALED TO ME HER WONDERS
BUT I HEARD THE OCEAN CREEP
I BURIED ALL MY TREASURE,
BURIED IN THE HOPELESS DEEP.

PARADISE, I LOST YOU
I'M CRYING OUT TO PARADISE ALONE.

I PLUNDERED AND I PILLAGED,

OH I PLOWED WITHOUT A CARE.
BUT THAT TREASURE—OH HER TREASURE,
I ALWAYS KNEW THAT IT WAS THERE.

AND IT CRIED FROM FAR OUT TO ME,
LIKE A THIEF IN THE NIGHT,
"YOU CAN'T RUN FROM A FEELING
FROM A HEART YOU KNOW IS RIGHT."

PARADISE, I LOST YOU
I'M CRYING OUT TO PARADISE ALONE.

SO I TURNED THE SHIP AND SAILED BACK
SAILED IT BACK TO FIND HER COAST.
BUT THE TREASURE OH MY TREASURE,
SHE WAS ONLY NOW A GHOST.

PARADISE, I LOST YOU
I'M CRYING OUT TO PARADISE ALONE.

PARADISE, I LOST YOU
I'M CRYING OUT TO PARADISE ALONE.

He ended with a strum of his guitar.

Hannah was moved to tears. "It's so good, Danny."

He smiled. "You're not the only one that likes it. I ran into an old friend the other day. He's starting an independent label. Thinks what I have is something worth getting behind. It's why I didn't come to you sooner. I didn't want to come with empty hands and no future. Plus, I had to cut off my phone service for a while to save some money." She laughed. "And now—well, I have something. Not much but…" He hesitated. "I want you to know I don't know how to even start being a dad…"

Hannah didn't try to wipe away the tears. "That's okay. They already have a dad. They just need their mom to be happy."

"I think I can help with that. And maybe I can even be a guy they want to be around—I like your kids. What do you say we give it a go?" He held out his hand.

"Danny, I want to say yes—you don't even know how much…"

"Hannah, we spent so much time trying to make things make sense. And they just didn't. None of it makes sense—not one damn bit. But I love you—and right now, other than my music—it's the only thing I have that's real."

Hannah put her hands to her mouth. "You love me? You never said that before."

"Hannah—I love you so much that it's a wonder I could write anything these past months, with how distracted I've been by my need to be with you again. You have been with me all this time, in my heart, in my head. Be with me in the flesh. Please." He put down the guitar.

"Using your old logic—it's not much to go on."

"It's not Hannah, I know—but it's everything that matters. I cannot hope to be worthy of you. But I will spend the rest of my life making up the past two years to you. I promise."

Hannah looked at him, looked at this man she had loved and who'd hurt her, with whom she'd shared a profound journey of self-discovery. And she found herself just wanting to be with him. "There's nothing to make up, Danny. All of that's done now." She walked over and he received her gratefully, holding her tight, as if he never wanted to let go. She felt his grasp and it gave her new life—life that was real and here and now. "Let's not waste any more time in the past."

"We'll look to the future," promised Danny.

"No—we'll look to right now. Because now is what we have. And I have a whole day to play hooky from work. Let's make it worth it." She grabbed his hand, smiling, and led him to the day that was there for them to cherish.

About the Author

Samantha Egret was born of a passion for writing and a desire to create an open dialog on female sexuality. She resides in Downtown Los Angeles, among the high-rises and large-living, a graduate of the high-stakes world of public relations. *Desire's Anthem* is her first novel.

Connect with Samantha at www.samanthaegret.com or www.facebook.com/samanthaegret.

www.ingramcontent.com/pod-product-compliance
Lightning Source LLC
Chambersburg PA
CBHW061209170626
46809CB00003B/1295